VERONICA GROVE

And Other Short Stories

WRITTEN BY
IVOR RAWLINSON

VERONICA GROVE

AND OTHER SHORT STORIES

IVOR RAWLINSON

The manufacturer's authorised representative in the EU
for product safety is Authorised Rep Compliance Ltd,
71 Lower Baggot Street, Dublin D02 P593 Ireland (www.arccompliance.com)

This is a work of fiction. Names, characters, businesses, places, events
and incidents are either the products of the author's imagination
or used in a fictitious manner. Any resemblance to actual persons,
living or dead, or actual events is purely coincidental.

Troubador Publishing Ltd
Unit E2 Airfield Business Park,
Harrison Road, Market Harborough,
Leicestershire. LE16 7UL
Tel: 0116 2792299
Email: books@troubador.co.uk
Web: www.troubador.co.uk

ISBN 978-1-83628-497-0

British Library Cataloguing in Publication Data.
A catalogue record for this book is available from the British Library.

Printed and bound in Great Britain by 4edge Limited
Typeset in 11pt Aldine401 BT by Troubador Publishing Ltd, Leicester, UK

For Emily, Alexis and Charlotte

CONTENTS

VERONICA GROVE

There are thirteen million dogs in Britain. If they all stood nose to tail, they would stretch from… well, let's just say a very long way. The residents of Veronica Grove, especially those near Clapham Common, would not be surprised to learn that thirty-one per cent of British households own a dog. Many residents are owners themselves and they swell the joyful stream of dogs being walked from Balham and Battersea to these special green spaces in South West London. It's said the nation wouldn't be half as healthy if it wasn't for the dogs that walk their owners twice a day. Dogs and their owners in this part of the world are undoubtedly fit. They are kings of the Common.

Of course, there are those in Veronica Grove (an unhappy minority) who dislike dogs. It's the same disgruntled minority that inveighs against electric scooters, rock concerts, side-by-side joggers and garden gnomes. Middle-class angst in the area, according to the local doctors, has reached alarming heights. Bin bags bulging with bottles like never before testify to the white wine after work *("Mummy's little helper")* and the whisky after dinner *("Daddy's wee dram")*.

When it comes to urban foxes, however, opinions are binary, for or against, and feelings run high. Lydia Bingham, living at number forty-eight – an attractive divorcee without any financial worries – accidentally stepped in a fox's poo as she was putting her bags in the bin before going to bed on a Thursday night last spring. She uttered an imprecation against the foxes with such force, such colour and so loudly that her neighbour opposite at number forty-seven opened his venetian blind – a rare event – to see what was happening. The next day, Lydia Bingham let rip on the Veronica Grove WhatsApp.

"Never," she wrote in Churchillian style, "never did I expect a fox to poo in my front garden. The smell and the mess are appalling. My suede slippers are soiled beyond redemption."

The WhatsApp reaction was predictably vociferous. There were nearly as many replies as there were to the unforgettable *"My Naughty Cat's Come Home"* thread last year. On the anti-fox side, a dozen individuals had been waiting for the opportunity to vent their spleen. Gregory, from number thirty-three, was ex-army, divorced and wanted a relationship with Lydia, but had been rebuffed. He doted on his rescue dog, a muscular German shepherd called Rambo, who suffered from post-traumatic stress disorder after ten years' sniffing for drugs for HM Customs and Excise. On walkies, Rambo was illegally let off the leash the moment he left the front door. Gregory said foxes had become more desperate since the introduction of locked compost bins and had even been seen stealing food deliveries. He couldn't understand why the council didn't do something. This prompted a typical reply from Harvey at number eighteen, who said the left-leaning council wouldn't do anything for a posh street like Veronica Grove. The most virulent anti-fox arguments came from Aidrian and Jeremy at number seventy, who said urban foxes had disgusting faeces, spread diseases and were vermin. "Residents should take matters into their own hands," they said.

The fox defenders had some powerful Establishment figures on their side. Jocelyn Waverley, an artist and, as he regularly pointed out, a member of the Royal Academy, wrote that foxes had as much right to share our world as we did, had a hard time finding food and should be protected. Geraldine Erskine-Jones, a life-time member of the RSPCA, wondered how vixens brought cubs into a hostile world such as in Clapham. She often put food out for her furry friends. Judy Steinbach, a solicitor, said foxes were persecuted just because they were foxes and they had a right to defend themselves.

Then came the dreadful discovery of that Saturday morning before Easter Sunday – two dead foxes on the pavement outside Lydia Bingham's front gate. They both had wounds on their necks. Lydia posted a picture on WhatsApp, begging someone to remove them. Gregory stepped forward, wearing army fatigues, leather boots, khaki woollen gloves and carrying what looked like army body bags. He circled the animals twice, perhaps to ensure they were dead, then, with impressive confidence and holding each fox by the tail, dropped them into separate body bags. By this time, a group of onlookers had built up. "Very courageous," pronounced Geraldine Erskine-

Jones, wiping away tears. Jocelyn Waverley, RA, clapped. Aidrian and Jeremy repeatedly said people shouldn't get too close. The assembled dog walkers kept their charges on tight leashes. Small children, returning from the Saturday morning kickabouts, were rushed past the gruesome sight by protective fathers.

On the bank holiday Monday, Lydia turned her usual book club meeting into what looked like the last act of an Agatha Christie murder mystery, when the suspects were brought together in her drawing room. All the ladies found seats and all the men stood around, rather awkwardly holding fine porcelain cups of awful coffee. Geraldine was wearing a distressed leather jerkin with a ban-the-bomb symbol faintly visible on the back. Judy Steinbach had brought much-thumbed copies of The Animal Welfare Act 2006 and the Wild Mammals (Protection) Act 1996. Jocelyn brought his dog, a beagle, who twice nipped Geraldine on the ankle. Jocelyn said he was just being playful.

Gregory was accompanied by Rambo and tethered him loosely to the lowest baluster of Lydia's staircase. It was Gregory who took charge of proceedings.

"Two crimes have been committed," he announced, as if addressing a parade. "First, the illegal elimination of two innocent foxes."

"Slaughter, I'd say," said Lydia.

"Secondly, the placing of their corpses in front of Lydia's front gate at night with the obvious intention of intimidating or frightening her. Unfortunately, she doesn't have a security camera. But can I ask you all to see if you have any footage that might be relevant? We can then call the police."

"You must be joking, Gregory," said Geraldine. "Not a hope in hell of the police doing anything."

Then, everyone tried to speak at once. "Not true." "Rubbish." "These foxes were shot." "There's a killer at large." "Frightened to go out at night." Wild accusations were made on all sides. Lydia's plate of chocolate digestives was knocked to the floor by Jocelyn's beagle. She quickly replaced it with a pre-sliced coffee and walnut cake. Harvey, who openly supported the Reform Party, said two foxes less in the street was not a big deal. "Balls," said Lydia loudly, which made the beagle yelp. The meeting was fast getting out of control.

"Hush," shouted Gregory. "We're forgetting why we're here. We shouldn't behave like a lynch mob. Laws have been broken and our hostess is a victim. Judy Steinbach is a solicitor. She's kindly brought along copies of the laws concerned. First, the death of the foxes," he boomed.

At the mention of foxes, Rambo pulled at his leash, broke the baluster and rushed into the sitting room. Tongue out, teeth bared, with his tail wagging wildly, he knocked the plate of coffee and walnut cake to the floor.

Lydia glowered. Gregory said, "Sorry everyone," then, "Bad dog, Rambo," and left the house.

"That dog's damaged, traumatised," said Lydia.

"So are we," said Jocelyn. And they all went home.

THE SUNBIRD
LODGE HOTEL

What struck Pascal Menard most when he first visited La Petite Côte were the colours and the quiet. The brightly painted *pirogues* drawn up on the beaches, with their fishing nets tucked inside them, flashed scarlet, orange and blue in the Senegalese sun. The marvellous mermaids, evil eyes and curling rollers on the boats had a wild style all of their own. The occasional vessel decorated in English football club colours didn't seem out of place. The names on them – Ayesha, Fatima, Bashir – were meant to bring luck to the fishermen, sometimes spending days and nights in the dangerous currents of the Atlantic.

As for the quietness of the coast, Pascal was comparing it to Dakar, seventy kilometres away, where he had a stressful job with Sengatel. He'd been with them for five years, after fifteen with the mother company in Paris. There were no noisy, clapped-out buses in these villages on either side of Popenguine, no terrifying taxis and, above all, no pointless hooting.

Pascal's out-of-office life revolved around cookery, tennis and religion. His meringues and macaroons were deservedly celebrated. They could even be the reason why he never married: few of his girlfriends could compete with his fabulous cooking.

One of the attractions of Popenguine, for Pascal, was the big, white-stone church, Notre-Dame de la Délivrande. He went for mass there. It was a place of pilgrimage for Catholics in otherwise Muslim Senegal. His faith was a counter-balance to his training as a computer scientist.

On his fourth visit to La Petite Côte, as he listened to the driver of a horse and cart singing on his way to deliver an outboard motor to the beach, he realised he wanted to be a part of this other world. In that magical moment, as the evening sun dipped into the ocean and as sandpipers picked up their supper on the foreshore, Pascal took the decision that would change his life.

He bought the Sunbird Lodge Hotel. Located one hundred metres up from the beach, in a village of some three hundred families where everyone smiled, the hotel – to put it mildly – had seen better days. Five bungalows slept in a sad semicircle around the main house, which had the all-important dining room and reception. Everything needed mending or repairing. Most windows didn't shut properly. Only half the creaking ceiling fans worked. Shutters had their slats missing. The showers were unpredictable. There was a musky odour of mosquito repellent in the bedrooms. Amazingly, though, there was an endless stream of faithful clients, and the financial accounts, handwritten in a school exercise book, showed the place made a healthy profit.

Moving from Dakar to the village was a truly African experience. Pascal's friends had wisely advised him not to accept the cheapest estimate from the removal people but the most expensive, contrary to the custom elsewhere. Watching the loading of his affairs onto a battered, open truck with tyres as smooth as a baby's bottom was bad enough. But following it as it lurched from side to side on the highway, then speeded up over the potholes as the driver neared his destination, was breathtaking.

It was widely believed in the village that the previous owner, Wafiq Ali, was mad. His rooms were behind reception. Mild-mannered and well-balanced until he bought the hotel and its staff ten years earlier, something flipped at the time of 'the big smell', when the cesspit overflowed and the whole place stank of dead fish. After that, he became increasingly eccentric. For example, his manager, Lamine Sene, claimed he'd been poisoned after they shared a dish of passion fruit and mangoes marinated in *buckeye* (home-made beer). In revenge, the manager deprived him of sleep by watching football on TV and blowing a whistle throughout each match. To get away from the whistling, he would sit in the wilderness at the back of the hotel, howling with frustration until curious jackals came out of the bush in answer to his calls. The last straw was when a troop of green monkeys, with their triangular faces and red eyes, took up residence in that same wilderness and the staff refused to shoo them away.

It was part of the hotel deal, Pascal discovered too late, that the existing staff – the manager, the cook, the gardener and three cleaners – stayed on. And the most important of these, of course, was the manager, Lamine Sene. Tall, handsome and nearing forty years old, Lamine had perfect teeth that positively sparkled when he spoke. He slept in the hotel reception and, while wielding immense power, mockingly deferred to both the old proprietor and later Pascal as 'Boss'.

When he was younger, he secretly ran a modestly successful business from the hotel as a shaman or witch doctor. Under the reception desk, he still kept the tools of his trade – lucky charms, amulets and a drum. Several jam jars contained herbs, berries and sand. Lamine used to heal, cast spells and communicate with the spirit world. He credited himself with Senegal's football team winning the Africa Cup. He was clearly not to be messed with.

Pascal's first week started well. Ramadan had just finished and the hotel hosted three happy Senegalese families, two courting couples and a German birdwatcher, who was dressed in camouflage day and night. But after this honeymoon week, things slipped out of Pascal's control. He felt he was resented not because he was French, but because of something else. At first, he couldn't put his finger on it. It was strange that nobody asked for more pay, for a start. When he tried to change the breakfast menu – apricot jam instead of baobab jelly – the cook took it as a personal insult. When he told the gardener to sweep the path, the gardener said it was beneath him. He would only do it if Lamine, and nobody else, told him to. When he found the cleaners were using can after can of insecticide spray followed by air freshener in each bedroom every day, they shrugged their shoulders and said Lamine liked it that way.

Pascal noticed that the hotel was attracting some strange types – mostly French, sad-looking, music-mad, lonesome folk who kept to their rooms. Some were regularly returning guests. They seemed to get on well with the locals and Pascal turned a blind eye to their entertaining of late-night visitors. Lamine, too, had a busy nightlife in reception. Pascal recognised most of them as fishermen and presumed they were bringing choice fish for Lamine and his friends, who were playing dominoes in the dining room until the small hours.

Difficulties really came to a head when Pascal told Lamine that he wanted to build a swimming pool in the wilderness behind the hotel. It would attract a better clientele. Profits would increase. Lamine half laughed, half grimaced, then shook his head. It would anger the *djinns*, the spirits. He would resign. The staff, too. And he would put a curse on Pascal.

"As for the profits, I'll let you into a little secret," Lamine said, while grabbing him by the arm behind the reception desk and pulling him towards him.

"This dump of a hotel is not making money – no money at all. But I'm making money. A lot of money. Look at this." He opened a suitcase with a combination lock. It was stuffed with banknotes.

"It's not fish that my friends are catching at night." His grip on Pascal's arm tightened. "They meet big fishing boats from Colombia, Guyana – so many places – and they buy packets of white powder for me, hundreds of packets a week." Lamine paused, then flashed his teeth at Pascal.

Three months later, Pascal bought a yacht and a brand-new Toyota Land Cruiser.

ROOM NINE

"I've never spoken into a microphone before. I'm glad you're sitting opposite me. You said you didn't want to interrupt and that I could talk for ten minutes. You'll have to make a signal or something to let me know when to stop.

"People seem to find my backstory particularly interesting. I think I know why. Both my parents were academics. They were both religious – Catholic – in an academic sort of way. My father had inherited enough money to send us both to a Catholic boarding school. Tragedy struck when I was sixteen, my brother seventeen. Our parents split up. They were more interested in their work than in us, it seemed. Anyway, that's the way I took it. I did really badly in my A levels, except art and woodwork. But I was seriously good at rugby.

"My father was ashamed of me, looking back on it. I needed to find myself somehow. I wanted to get away from everything. I had a school friend who was going to Florence to learn Italian and I asked if I could join him. My father wanted to see the back of me, so willingly financed me for a three-month language course there. I had a wonderful time. I found a weekend job as a waiter in a *trattoria* near where I was living, just off the Via de' Pandolfini. I had a free supper two days a week. But, more importantly, I often used to walk round the corner to the *Badia Fiorentina* monastery, with its cool, quiet church. It was a great place to contemplate.

"In Florence, I met the girl of my dreams – Magdalena. She was warm and funny and puckered her lips ever so slightly when she smiled, like this. She'd bought a Vespa and at weekends I'd fill my backpack with bread, ham, cheese, grapes and Chianti, and we'd seek out heavenly picnic spots. We tried to speak to each other only in Italian. We'd sometimes fall asleep in each other's arms and awake as the shadows lengthened over landscapes of olive groves, vineyards and cypresses that hadn't changed for thousands of years.

"Oh, you're signalling to me. Irrelevant? That I should speed up, right? OK. I will.

"After I came back from Italy, my year's perfect happiness ended abruptly. There was no family home to go to because both our parents had found other partners with their own houses. My brother had found work in Canada and stayed there. And Magdalena's parents made it clear that I was unworthy of their daughter; that I had no qualifications and no prospects. I had just enough money for a room in Earl's Court. Discovered it on a website. Through friends, I found a job in the basement of a gallery in Fulham Road making picture frames. All the time, I was hoping that I could redeem myself in the eyes of Magdalena's parents, but it wasn't to be. And at her job in TV news, she was swept away by admirers in a matter of weeks. I never really got over it.

"I don't know why – for consolation, perhaps – I went to the Isle of Wight on a long weekend retreat to Quarr Abbey. You probably haven't heard of it, but it's a beautiful place with an unusual history. Benedictine monks. It's modern – well, early 1900s on the site of a large twelfth-century monastery. And, curiously, the new monastery's first inhabitants in 1906 were French. They were fleeing from the anti-clerical French government of the time and given sanctuary there. The monks now are English. I was in a bad place mentally at that moment. At Quarr, I immediately forgot about my dysfunctional family, about my shattered love life and my money troubles. To cut a long story short – I can see you nodding approval – I was accepted as a novice and after probation was prepared to devote the rest of my life to God.

"I suppose only those who have this vocation, this calling, can understand. I felt an almost physical pull. It was something very special – transcendent, all-embracing, like coming home having been lost. I dare say most people are never able to permanently inhabit the spiritual dimension that lies within all of us. It's what distinguishes us from robots, isn't it? I haven't time nor the words to describe the mystery of faith. But my Benedictine brothers and I lived in communion with a higher power than any on earth. At the same time, we were grounded because we ran a farm, did religious teaching, ran a small gift shop and a bookbinding operation. At lunch, one of us read aloud to the rest of us – history, biographies, foreign affairs. We knew what was going on in the world. There were nine of us at the beginning of my probation in 2020. But tragedy struck once more when, first, our revered, much-loved abbot, then all the rest of us, caught Covid. The abbot was eighty-two and never recovered. Services were no longer open to the public at the abbey. His death led to a sadness; a feeling of instability and insecurity. We could no longer worship or work as we wanted. Covid left us with mental problems. Three of us left at the same time to seek professional help.

"I had a brilliant therapist, who quickly realised I needed to find a job with a structure, where I could think my own thoughts and with a spiritual dimension. But any job also had to keep me in touch with people, with the real world. He suggested I live in a flat owned by a Catholic charity attached to a convent in South London.

"I was incredibly lucky finding my present job. I wanted something without stress but where I could be of service. The advertisement said they were looking for people who were professional and punctual; able to remain alert for a whole shift; enforce rules in a courteous manner; assist in collecting information. I had two interviews and they did a thorough police check on me. The National Gallery is huge and I started work in the Sainsbury Wing. The guarding duties were only a part of the job. One had to answer questions about the location of pictures in the gallery, where the exit was, the toilets (a very popular question). The gallery knew I had lived in Florence, spoke Italian and was a committed Christian, and I was delighted when I was moved to Room 9, *Renaissance Old Masters*.

"Because Room 9 holds the National Gallery's greatest treasure – Leonardo's *The Virgin of the Rocks*, there are normally three attendants. It was shocking for me to see how little attention the crowds of visitors paid to the pictures. They were meaningless to the majority. Actually, I prefer Bronzino's *The Madonna and Child with Saints.* I spent literally hours looking at it. Bronzino's *Madonna* reminded me of my Magdalena: exquisite.

"Oh, you're tapping your watch again. It all happened so fast. The man was wearing a suit, which was unusual but you never know, do you? I noticed him because he kept looking at the Veroneses, then the Titian, then the Bronzino again. He twice looked to see where I was sitting but avoiding my eyes. When he pulled an envelope out of his inside pocket together with something orange, I took no chances. How could I know it was a handkerchief?

"Anyway, I threw myself at him from behind, shouting, 'Oh no you don't,' or something. These Just Stop Oil protesters had been targeting the Derby, the Grand National, Lord's – you name it. Throwing orange powder at my Bronzino would have been quite possible. I hit him with my shoulder behind his knees and he fell forward and that triggered the alarm. Perfect rugby tackle.

"He was furious when he'd recovered and saw that I was an attendant. I had no idea who he was. I apologised profusely but it wasn't enough. Someone had to be blamed and it was me. I was dismissed. I was the scapegoat, I suppose.

"I cannot say I liked the headline in one of the tabloids the next day: *Ex-Monk Fells Director of National Gallery.*"

THE WOODS

Every French village has one. Someone who is the village memory; who has lived there longer than anyone else and who remembers things like the drunken hunter who shot Madame Valmy's chickens fifty years ago. In our case, it was a former author, Marcel, long since deceased. He was retired when I first knew him; a slightly mysterious figure, usually unshaven, but otherwise well dressed, a smoker, who lived alone. I would meet him first at the *tabac* buying *Le Monde* with his cigarettes, then in the café, endlessly stirring a *café crème.*

Given half a chance, he would chat non-stop. During the war, he was a teenager in the village where we lived. According to Marcel, his father had been quite prominent in the Resistance. I hate people going on about the war. As far as I'm concerned, the page has been turned and we need to look forwards, not backwards. But I do remember Marcel saying, several times, in a whisper, "You wouldn't believe what happened in the woods during the war. And after all, they were all French, turning against each other, calling each other traitors and so on." I always changed the conversation, but the teenage boy had clearly been traumatised and couldn't forget whatever it was.

That's by-the-by. Fast forward to last October. My wife, Claudine, and I had had some bad luck financially. The savings we'd had, never a lot in the first place, had been spent on completely re-making our roof, which was full of woodworm. Then, our car packed up. "Rusted chassis; worth nothing now," said the man in the village garage. The final straw was our labrador's illness. The vet's fees for treating his heart were astronomical, but he was still a young dog, so we paid to keep him alive.

Walking in the hills around the village was one of the few pleasures left to us and it cost nothing. A week before the dreaded Hallowe'en – on a Friday, as I recall – it was one of those typical autumn days: windy, changeable, flying clouds alternating with royal-blue sky, with air so pure you felt it should be bottled and sold. We decided to walk to La Pérouse on the path through the woods. It normally took us about two hours. There was a bus back every hour.

I remember that, unusually, I took a walking stick – the heavy one I inherited from my grandfather. Claudine, bless her heart, took just a plastic bag for the chestnuts. When we crossed the bubbling, bouncing stream at the bottom of the village, the weather was alright.

One can see why our ancestors had built a watermill down there – a perfect waterfall, good tracks for horses and carts and the village close by. Our track for La Pérouse was sunken and probably very old. It first went uphill between steep fields close-cropped by goats, then downhill for a bit with prickly hawthorn hedges on either side, full of chattering blue tits on that particular day. At the top of the track, pieces of wet quartz glistened and flashed in the stuttering sunlight. Lower down, there were big puddles where we usually picked blackberries that were as sweet as honey.

To the right, hidden from view, is an old silver and lead mine on the side of the hill. It dates back to Gallo-Roman times, maybe earlier. The Romans used the lead from it for pipes on their aqueducts. It fell into disrepair, was reworked in the seventeenth century and then abandoned again.

Claudine and I had more than a sneaking admiration for the Romans. It's silly, I know, but I was often aware of their presence in the woods beside parts of the aqueduct. Remains of their work were scattered along the path we were taking. The area is full of freshwater springs. What confidence they must have had to have even considered transporting that water from seven different directions for 30, 40 or even 80 plus kilometres in one case, from the springs to their then capital city, Lyons, which they called Lugdunum. How brilliant their engineers were to have built the siphons to send the water across valleys! What precision they needed to ensure the water always ran at the same speed! How artistic they were in their use of brick and tile on the majestic, high arches of the aqueduct, all perfectly aligned, when it ran over low ground. One can understand why, far to the north, the Anglo-Saxons described their Roman remains as the work of giants.

There had been gales and two days of heavy rain at the beginning of the week. Golden leaves and twigs were everywhere and the path was carpeted in chestnuts. Many husks had burst open, revealing one big nut and two smaller ones, shining in shafts of autumn sun, as if they had just been washed. I used my stick and my foot to make them pop out, then stuffed them into my pockets. They were a staple and free food for our ancestors, who sometimes made them into flour, sometimes into a purée or paste. We just roasted them in the fireplace and their smell when slightly burnt was as much a part of our lives as our log fires or frost.

Claudine and I seldom argue. But we did that day. For one thing, I was tired after just an hour. For another, I could see a storm brewing. Fluffy white clouds had given way to low, dark-grey ones and the wind direction had changed.

"Let's turn back," I said. "We're going to get soaked."

"Why turn back when we're halfway there?" said Claudine.

As if to prove my point, there was an enormous, ear-splitting crack of thunder, followed three seconds later by a flash of lightning that seemed to be only metres away. Then the rain started. Heavy, drenching, cold rain.

"We could get home faster," Claudine said, "if we cut through the woods, past *Le Grand Rocher*." It's a wonderful lookout point when the weather's fine.

"No way am I going through the woods in a thunderstorm. It's dangerous. You know that. I'll keep to the path." Truth to tell, the lightning had spooked me. The woods looked dark and unfriendly.

"Do as you want," said Claudine. "I bet I'll be home before you." Her curly hair was bedraggled; rain dripped off her eyebrows. There was no point in trying to dissuade her.

And with that, she was gone. I stood still on the path for a moment while she rustled off through the leaves and branches.

I arrived home about an hour later, wet through, with rain somehow dripping down my back. My fingers were cold and I struggled to take off my muddy boots before opening the door. I could see Claudine had already returned because her plastic bag was on the table. Not only that, but she had also showered and put on dry clothes. I was ready to be humiliated, I suppose. But she skipped to the door, hugged me, kissed me on the nose, then stood back with a smile from ear to ear.

"Guess what I found in the woods? You won't believe it. Look." She led me to the kitchen and pointed to not one, but two fist-sized black truffles.

"I've weighed them. Just under a kilo each. I've looked it up: 1500 euros each. And there are several more where the trees have been blown over."

We opened our last bottle of *Saint-Émilion Grand Cru* that night. I'd been keeping it for a special occasion.

THE GP

My neighbour, Len, lost his wife, Margaret, tragically to Covid in 2020. Margaret was my patient, but Len wasn't. I didn't know him well. 'Hello' or 'Good morning' and that was it. He kept himself to himself. I never knew about his background.

I kept meaning to check on Len after his wife's death. I thought he might be lonely. I had many patients who were. Loneliness is not a jolly business. It creeps up on you little by little, like arthritis. At first, people deny they are lonely as if there's a stigma attached to it, like Aids. They don't talk to others for days at a time. They talk to themselves. They watch daytime TV. And they ask questions of their pets – "What do you think about the Middle East, Rufus?" – holding the animal's front paws. Pets are pleasantly surprised by this new-found attention. Most have never been consulted on global political issues.

Covid was unbelievably stressful for GPs like me. As the only unmarried male doctor in the practice, I was working crazy hours without anyone at home telling me to stop. We are already forgetting what frightening and desperate times those were. Personally, I thought the most worrying aspect was that we were really not sure how Covid was transmitted. And, of course, there were terrible shortages of, and battles for, protective kit of all sorts. A year into the pandemic, I was living on adrenaline like a marathon runner. The discovery of the vaccines was utterly brilliant.

I see now that I became too emotionally engaged with vulnerable patients, like Len's wife, Margaret. She was a long-time asthma sufferer and had a dodgy heart. She didn't stand a chance when both her lungs were infected, but she put up such a brave fight. Len couldn't be with her at the end. He had to be content – how cruel – with a video call on a kind nurse's mobile. I felt sick when the hospital told me all this and said how sorry they were. I expected to talk to Len by phone, but he never rang and I was overwhelmed with urgent cases.

I hate consultations by phone. It's impossible to pick up the little signs of mental issues, domestic abuse, alcohol problems, depression and loneliness. Especially with young people – the sixteen- to twenty-year-olds – who have all the difficulties of transitioning from school to a next step. They have pressures we tend to dismiss and are sometimes inarticulate. The pandemic turned hundreds of my patients' lives upside down. Long covid was a sinister reality and we didn't have the time nor expertise to deal with it.

I was in denial about my own health and stability. I guess I thought I was invulnerable. I decided to refuse to work on weekends.

So it was that on a Saturday morning in the spring of 2021, I, at last, had time to chat to Len over the garden fence. I was impressed by the way he was giving his front garden a makeover. He had built a wooden box for the dustbins and had put three olive trees in black planters parallel with the pavement. He had repainted the red front door and polished the brass door furniture until it twinkled. I was worried that Len was preparing the terraced house for sale. Selfishly, I thought that would mean building works for months. Often, the first thing wealthy City folk do is to dig out their basements. I know of one house in our street where the lawyer-owner spent half a million making a 'basement' that extended down his back garden! Above all, I felt guilty that I hadn't checked on Len before now. I asked him how he was doing on his own.

"Not too bad, really," he said. "Margaret and I always intended to do work on the house. But I never got round to it, you know how it is."

I nodded. "Well, I must say you're doing a fantastic job. Makes a lot of difference."

"It keeps my mind off other things." He paused and took a deep breath. "Dear Margaret was like a squirrel. She collected things and then sort of hid them."

At that point, my mobile rang. It was the hospital and, out of habit, I answered. I still hadn't logged out of work mentally. I could feel Len wanted to talk. But he waited a few moments, then went indoors.

The week that followed was dreadful for me. I felt nothing was going in the right direction with the pandemic. I was utterly exhausted. Two of my patients were in intensive care and I wondered whether I could have dealt with their cases differently. We were all getting criticised in the surgery. The biggest complaint was that patients simply couldn't get appointments with us. We were overwhelmed.

Early on, we had stopped patients making appointments at the front desk in person, but we had not yet fully moved to online booking. The receptionists were being abused regularly on the phone. Yet it was with one of them that I lost my temper, on a Friday afternoon, for not passing on a phone message from intensive care at the hospital. A colleague overheard me and suggested I go home and get some sleep. I asked someone to take over my list for the rest of the day. I shut down my terminal and walked home.

I slept for fourteen hours, with a little pharmaceutical assistance. In sunshine the next morning, I heard Len whistling beautifully as he put another coat of paint on his front door.

He smiled as I picked up my only newspaper of the week from the doorstep. We talked about spring, about collecting, about cricket, and then he said:

"You've had a rough week, haven't you, doctor?"

"How do you know? I have, actually. Very rough. And not just a week."

"Come in for a coffee. I have to leave the door ajar to let the paint dry. So, when you're dressed, just walk in."

Half an hour later, in Len's comfortable, tidy kitchen, we were breakfasting. He must have known that I would come round that morning. I thought I was in doctor-patient mode and that he needed help. But he took me completely by surprise by stopping my questions, putting his hand on my forearm and announcing that he had been a GP himself. I was the one who needed help, he said. He'd noticed the silly hours I was working because his bedroom was in the front of the house and he had heard my front door closing at six in the morning and at ten-thirty at night.

In his living room, two armchairs had been set up in front of a sizeable TV.

"Thought you would like to watch the cricket with me. There's veal and ham pie for lunch and four bottles of real ale in the fridge."

I flopped into the armchair, practically speechless with surprise and joy. There was a bigger surprise to come.

"I've been talking to your surgery partners for a couple of days. I'm starting as a locum on Monday. I've maintained my GMC registration, been revalidated and my licence to practice is okay. Ever since I saw, for myself, with poor Margaret, how impossibly stretched the health service was by this pandemic, I'd been wondering how I could help. I've said I'll start on a monthly basis but that will depend on you to a large extent."

"On me?" I asked.

"Yes. The partners will tell you either today or tomorrow that they want you to step back, to take a break. I'll take the strain."

After lunch, I fell fast asleep again, watching the cricket and rejoicing in the kindness of neighbours.

DRUNK AND DISORDERLY

In the corridor outside the courtroom, the lady usher could see that Justin was nervous. He was fidgeting with the knot on his carefully chosen blue tie and constantly running his hand through his longish, wavy grey hair.

"There will be three people on the bench this morning – two women on either side of Peter McAdam. The women are legally trained and give advice on matters of law to the magistrate," she explained.

"Would that be Sir Peter McAdam, a trustee of The Old Vic?"

The usher looked puzzled. She wasn't the theatre-going type. "No idea," she said. "Your case is the first to be heard. Better to be first, don't you think? Less waiting around. Where's your solicitor?"

"I don't have one. I'm defending myself," Justin said. He thought of making a witty remark on the lines of 'With a name like Justin…' but quickly thought better of it.

"I don't need to tell a gentleman like yourself to stand up when making your case."

"Of course," said Justin, automatically straightening his back.

He was disappointed inside the courtroom to see how modern and business-like it all looked with computer screens everywhere. Pictogram notices showed that mobile phones were prohibited. There was a smell of air freshener. A dead fly, on its back, was on Justin's chair. He took this to be an ill omen. There were five members of the public and an earnest-looking journalist. The prosecuting police officer was even more earnest. He never stopped looking at his computer screen.

Matters started awkwardly. The magistrate asked for Justin's full name and address.

"Justin Bradbury, Sir. Flat C, 10 Colin Street, Chelsea, London, SW3."

The magistrate looked at his screen again, then at the policeman. "Ah. On the charge sheet, we have Joseph Binford."

"That was my name, Sir. Indeed, I suppose it still is, in a way. My name now, my stage name, is Justin Bradbury."

"Stage name?"

"I'm an actor, Sir. A strolling player. My agent, some forty years ago now, thought Justin Bradbury was more… masculine."

"I'm glad we've cleared that up, Mr… Binford…" The magistrate spat the name out as if it were distasteful. "There are three charges against you. All date from 1am on Tuesday 6th of August this year. First, being drunk and disorderly. Second, disturbing the peace. And third, threatening to assault a police officer. How do you plead?"

"Not guilty on all counts, Sir."

The young policeman started by saying that he wasn't the police officer involved on that night. It was his colleague, who was now on indefinite sick leave.

"As a result of injuries sustained on 6th August?" enquired the magistrate.

"No, Sir. His nerves had gone long before that."

The magistrate looked over his glasses, unhappy about something. But he told the police officer to carry on. The officer tilted his computer screen too brusquely and his overfilled water glass spilt onto his desk. The usher leapt forward and mopped it up. The officer spoke in a flat monotone and stumbled over words like 'inebriated', 'sufficient *prima facie* evidence' and 'urinating aggressively'. But he made a good case. It made Justin out to be a dangerous menace, a hooligan and disrespectful of authority.

Sir Peter McAdam turned to Justin, looking at him like a specimen flushed out of a drain. He couldn't say he was revolted, but it showed.

"This is the first time, Sir, that I've been before a magistrate and I bitterly regret it. Putting you all to so much trouble. There were, if I may say so, mitigating circumstances. Our play at the Royal Court was a brilliant satire on the upper classes between the wars. But the three or four theatre critics that really matter in London didn't understand it and panned it, so that it was doomed from the first night. It was taken off after a week, on the 6th of August. I was booed that night. First time in my whole career. I don't know if you can imagine what that is like for an actor. It shows contempt and it hurts."

"We haven't got time to discuss the fate of a play at

the Royal Court or anywhere else. Or actors' feelings, Mr Binford. Just address the charges."

But Justin couldn't avoid playing to the gallery, especially now that he knew about the magistrate's association with The Old Vic.

"The cast at the Royal Court had a melancholy, rather intense, after party when the curtain came down for the last time. I walked home later perfectly normally. I even remember, in the King's Road, dancing the waltz from the play's last act as I hummed 'The Blue Danube'."

The journalist giggled and started writing in his notebook.

"In my humble opinion, Sir Peter, there are several states of intoxication, rather like the seven ages of man in *As You Like It*, and they range from tipsy to paralytic. I was tiddly, woozy or squiffy, but not, Sir, definitely not tanked or stonking drunk. For example, I was perfectly able to converse with people in the street and dance without falling over. And as for disorderly, this is surely wholly subjective. One man's disorder might be another man's genius. Take Oscar Wilde."

At this, the magistrate put his head in his hands and said, "I beg you, Mr Binford, do not digress. The prosecution statement says the police officer heard you singing raucously while urinating over his shoes in the front garden of 10 Colin Street as he tried to arrest you."

"I was trained to sing at RADA, Sir Peter, and my rendering of 'O Sole Mio' is my party piece. But, as I recall, I was singing the National Anthem, as I often do at night, when the police officer strode into my front garden. I do admit, I was spending a penny then. Nature cannot be denied, can it, Sir? It was uncommonly urgent and could not wait. The officer was shouting at me and this attracted the notice of a passing taxi driver, who called out loud, "Rule Britannia," and gave me the thumbs up. As I turned to face the intruder, no doubt some piddle fell on his shoes. No harm was meant. As for disturbing the peace, there is none – none at all – to be disturbed on Colin Street, a rat-run between King's Road and Fulham Road." Justin buttoned the jacket of his velvet suit and stood tall. "I suggest, Sir, that it is highly significant that the police officer's nerves had gone long ago. It must be a stressful job. But may I also ask, Sir, since when is it illegal for an Englishman to pee in his own front garden? And since when, Sir, was it illegal to sing the National Anthem in the Royal Borough of Kensington and Chelsea?"

Sir Peter shook his head sadly twice and said in a clear voice, "Case dismissed."

DARK MATTER

George Randall's pilgrimage to Pune had been hugely successful. For years, he'd been eager to see where his grandfather in India had lived from 1903 to 1935. He had married there and George's father had been born there. He wrote many books about Indian history and culture, taught in three colleges and was finally principal of Deccan College in Poona, now Pune. George had been unsure, when arranging the visit to the university, how he would be received. His grandfather, although liberal, unconventional and enlightened, was nevertheless a man of his time – a believer in the rightness of the British Empire. Pune was a major centre of resistance to the British Raj and who knows whether George's grandfather's sympathy for Indian independence was understood by the Indian militants or whether he was hated. In Pune, George was dealing with academics and the pre-visit correspondence could not have been more friendly. He had been garlanded as he stepped off the train from Mumbai and offered every possible courtesy on the campus. He was genuinely moved by the respect with which the present-day principal talked of his colonial predecessor.

Pune, a hundred miles inland from Mumbai, has no less than nine universities, including the largest in the country. Some of the colonial architecture still stands – the Anglican church, the bungalows, the railway station. They reflect the unique blend of the old and the new that makes India so special. The college that welcomed George, and the man he later met in the train, illustrated this perfectly.

The college was a step back in time, with its Victorian Gothic buildings, arches, arcades and a tower. Its focus was on time past. It had become a small research institute with three departments – ancient history and archaeology; linguistics; Sanskrit and lexicography. In a large room filled with boxes of index cards, scholars were compiling a definitive dictionary of Sanskrit. They said it would be many years before it was finished. Even though Sanskrit had not been spoken for centuries, the lexicographers were utterly convincing about the importance of the language for India's religions and culture.

The chance meeting with Dr Ranjit Chandra on the train back to Mumbai was a complete contrast and a career changer. He was a scientist whose focus was far in the future. He had obviously been on this train before. He knew straight away where his reserved seat was and exactly how to make himself comfortable. When he saw George struggling with the window blind, he said, "I wouldn't bother if I were you, my friend. Very few of the blinds work. And sometimes it's best not to look out of the window anyway. Gives people vertigo, especially at Bhore Ghat –

the mountain pass. I'm Ranjit Chandra, by the way." He leant across and shook George's hand.

"George Randall. Thank you. I won't bother with the blind then."

"The line from Bombay to Poona was built in the 1850s. Thousands of workers died constructing it, especially the tunnels. It took nine years."

"About the same time as the high-speed line we're building in England from London to Birmingham."

"Ah, Birmingham," Ranjit said. "I spent a year at Jodrell Bank, commuting from Manchester."

"So, you're a scientist then."

"Yes. An astrophysicist, to be exact. And you?"

"Writer. Fiction, mostly. Some short stories. And children's books."

Dr Chandra paused for a while, then said, "I've often thought we don't have the vocabulary in any language to describe the universe. At the astrophysics centre in Pune, we're working at the very edge of knowledge. Take dark matter. It's hypothetical. We don't *know* for sure it exists, but we *think* so because it has a gravitational effect on visible matter."

"Can't mathematics describe these things?"

"To some extent, yes. But astrophysicists are reluctant to put their equations into words. Our giant radio telescope north of Pune is detecting radio waves emitted by celestial objects that are inexplicable according to the laws of nature."

"So, we must reconsider the laws of nature?"

"Yes. We are doing so on an almost weekly basis as we study dark matter, black holes and time. Time and space must be defined differently. The slowing of time near a black hole is extreme. One year near a black hole could be the equivalent of eighty years on earth. It stops altogether at the event horizon."

"Event horizon?"

"It's the one-way boundary of a black hole, which traps light. It marks the point where the gravitational pull is so strong that nothing can escape."

"Difficult to imagine that – for me, at least," said George.

"It's actually upsetting," said Dr Chandra. "It's intellectually troublesome. We need writers to help us grapple with articulating these new concepts."

"I'd like to help," George said. "Seriously. I'm between books at the moment."

Their conversation was interrupted by an announcement apologising profusely for the train being an hour late.

"Indian railways have their own concept of time," a smiling Dr Chandra said.

As the train drew into Victoria Terminus, Mumbai, he pointed at the platform. People were cooking and eating in groups. A girl in full bridal dress, sparkling with sequins, was incongruously carrying a heavy black plastic bag – her dowry, perhaps? Boys ran alongside the train with outstretched hands, begging. Two turbaned Sikhs were lifting a very old man in a wheelchair up some steps. Hot food of all types was on sale. There were good smells of incense and curry. And bad smells of cow dung and cardboard being burnt.

"Every now and then, I need to reconnect with reality," Dr Chandra said.

The train came to a halt with squealing brakes and the two men exchanged email addresses. Dr Chandra's visiting card said, 'Director, National Centre for Astrophysics, Pune'.

Armed with a five-year work permit, George sometimes worked with Dr Chandra but otherwise was left to find the words to go beyond the edge of knowledge. It was a huge challenge. He sympathised with the Sanskrit lexicographers.

And he often thought of John Donne's lines:

And new philosophy calls all in doubt,
The element of fire is quite put out;
The sun is lost, and th'earth, and no man's wit,
Can well direct him where to look for it.

AT THE EDGE

It was ten days before Christmas and bitterly cold. Stephen was taking his daily walk to buy a newspaper and – a last-minute request from Diane – some stamps. People walking towards the underground station leant into the wind with hunched shoulders like the figures in a Lowry painting. Halfway there, on the corner by the tennis courts, Stephen saw a fit-looking man, wearing a cream-coloured anorak and a white baseball cap with 'AJS' embroidered on it, with two dogs on leads.

The man stopped when he reached Stephen. "Hello. How are you?" he said.

Stephen's brain raced. It drew a blank, so he replied, "Do I know you?"

"No, you don't. We haven't met before but I just thought I'd say hello. I hope you don't mind. My name's Thomas." He held out his hand. It was large, his grip was firm and his nails were well trimmed.

"I'm Stephen Reed. Do you often talk to strangers?"

"More and more. I think we all walk on by too much. You looked interesting and your red scarf triggered something. People like to be acknowledged."

Fearing that this was a nutter, Stephen turned to go. But curiosity got the better of him and he took the bait. "Why do I look interesting?" he said, feeling a bit foolish.

"Deep in thought. Hands behind your back. If there were ice, I'd say you were skating," Thomas said with a broad smile.

"Actually, there is some black ice," said Stephen. "And I find that keeping my hands behind my back eases my backache."

"Ah. Sporting injury?"

"No. Something else." Stephen hesitated. He wished he'd worn an extra sweater. The wind was blowing the dogs' ears inside out. Snow was in the air.

Something about Thomas' strong physique, the set of implanted top teeth and the stand-out muscles sloping from his neck to his shoulders made Stephen ask if he played rugby by any chance.

"I did, as it happens. Which is why your red scarf caught my attention. Same colour exactly as my rugby shirts."

"So, Wales then?"

"Yes. Modesty should forbid. But I played three times for Wales. Scrum half. Had to give it up when my knees went, one after another. I miss it so much."

"That's amazing. What do you miss most?"

Thomas tugged on the peak of his ridiculous baseball cap, then said, "Living on the edge. At international level, you push yourself to the absolute limit. The stakes are incredibly high. Fame and fortune if you succeed. Ignominy and derision if you fail. The whole country is watching. It's do or die when you wear the red shirt."

The two dogs were getting restless. Thomas wanted to finish his answer.

"There's a pride about playing for Wales that is difficult to describe. We're only a little country but we're proud, you know?"

Stephen could hear the lilt in his voice as he said it. "Are you still playing at all?" Stephen asked.

"Sadly, no. Fortunately, I had a second string to my bow. I'm a singer with the Welsh Opera."

"No more living on the edge," Stephen said.

"On the contrary. Probably more! The build-up is the same in the dressing room of the opera house as in the dressing room at the stadium. Waiting for the curtain to go up after the overture is every bit as exciting as waiting for the ref to blow his whistle for the beginning of the match. Opera and rugby are both performances. Both are about artistry."

At that moment, a heavily built young man on one of those electric bikes with a big box over the rear wheel came from the direction of the shops and took the corner way too fast. He skidded and fell practically in front of Thomas and Stephen. The dogs jumped and yelped. The cyclist swore. There was a red trail on the black ice.

Both men ran to pick him up. It disgusted Stephen to see the dogs licking the stuff off the roadway until he saw that it wasn't blood but tomato sauce, or something from the pizza in the cyclist's now broken box.

"Are you alright?" said Stephen.

"I think so," said the cyclist, pulling the hood of his anorak down. A couple of male joggers briefly stopped on the other side of the road, looked at the scene, concluded that no more help was needed and resumed their jog.

Fortunately, there was a bench on the corner. When Thomas and Stephen saw that the skin had been scraped off the palm of the cyclist's hand, they persuaded him to sit down and patch it up with the help of two clean handkerchiefs. Stephen had fully expected the cyclist to be Albanian or Syrian, so was surprised to discover that he was English, was doing a doctorate on artificial intelligence at Imperial College and was delivering pizzas as a vacation job. Before telling the two men any more, he phoned the pizza place, asked for someone else to deliver the order and said the box on the bike was broken. The boss wasn't happy but the cyclist said that he wouldn't be sacked because he was the fastest rider they'd ever had.

"They're proud of their boast that they'll get a pizza delivered from oven to door in this postcode within six minutes, twenty-four/seven. It's a challenge – a personal challenge for the riders. I suppose I have an accident every two days or so. I wasn't counting on ice on the road this late in the day."

"You'll need some antiseptic on your hand," Stephen said. "Couldn't you find a more comfortable vacation job – in a pub, for example?"

"Or teaching non-tech people like me how to make more of their mobiles and organise their work properly on their laptops. The demand for help like that must be huge," said Thomas while Stephen nodded hard.

"Probably could," said the cyclist. "But delivering pizzas suits me. I like meeting the customers. I like getting to know the other deliverers. They've got amazing stories to tell of their journeys to the UK. There's a real camaraderie. The money's not brilliant, but sometimes the tips are, especially at Christmas. I like the exercise and fresh air." He put his hood over his head as if to go. "Actually, most of all, I like the speed and the risk. It's what attracted me to artificial intelligence. Working at the frontier of our understanding. With both delivering pizzas and AI, we're living at the edge, aren't we?" He laughed as he said it. "By the way, thanks so much for your help."

He picked up his bike and rode off. It started to snow.

A DAY'S DRIVE

Raimond had never been on holiday in all of his forty-five years. He liked it in the village where he was. The same man (it had always been a man) had been elected mayor for the past thirty-two years – a sure sign of common happiness. The *Café de la Poste* had never changed its name, even though there hadn't been a post office in Saint Florian since 1959. Going to Toulouse, the nearest city, was always an unpleasant experience except when he went to watch the rugby. Otherwise, it meant bureaucracy, or the bank, or getting lost. Raimond couldn't understand why others didn't feel like he did about holidays; why supposedly intelligent people should drive from one end of Europe to the other to live in tents.

Raimond owned a garage. When his father had run it, it was a petrol station with two pumps. It was now a tractor dealership and servicing garage, mostly for specialised vineyard tractors with low centres of gravity, tight turning circles and hydraulic pumps for spraying. The garage was as important to Saint Florian as the Co-op or the café and hotel owned by his sister, Lucille. Almost as important, jokers would say, as the *piste de boules* under the plane tree in front of the mayor's grand house (illegally refurbished with local authority funds, so they say).

Tractors were vital for the vineyards, now that labour was so scarce. Other things hadn't changed for years. The rituals were the same. Ploughing, fertilising, pruning, picking, pressing – and the whole village prospered. But for the past few years, things had started to go wrong. And they weren't things that could easily be put right, like dealing with aphids or fungus. The first thing was that the market for French wine outside France was faltering in the face of New World wine, which was more competitive and more to the taste of foreigners. And the young were drinking more beer than wine. This wasn't just happening in rugby-mad South West France, but everywhere. But much more of a threat was climate change. Mid-summer dry spells had become months-long droughts. Hot sunshine had become heatwaves, which burnt bunches of burgeoning grapes to biscuit brown. When it did rain, it came all at once and more frequently than ever in ferocious thunderstorms, washing the soil away. When there was hail, now more common than ever, the hailstones were sometimes the size of walnuts, devastating the grapes. Saint Florian's fortunes faltered.

Help was at hand from an unexpected quarter. Like moths attracted to a flame, tourists couldn't resist the call of the sun, the markets, the food – the way of life in South West France. Their number swelled as their once-favoured, more exotic destinations in North Africa, Turkey or the Middle East became too risky. French TV news played its part, too, by devoting hours each week to France's golden beaches, sapphire seas and majestic mountains.

Manfred Glassbrenner, his partner, Gunda, and their sixteen-year-old son, Leo, shattered the calm of Saint Florian – and shattered is not too strong a word – in the last weekend of April. They had been driving their small camper van – the millennium model with the roof that opens like a bellows – all the way from Frankfurt. It was a tough drive to Saint-Antonin-Noble-Val, their eventual destination, at the best of times. But this was a holiday weekend and the motorways, seen from a drone, were like a continuous ribbon of steel. So, when the GPS on Manfred's phone suggested an alternative route, completely avoiding motorways, the day's driving plan was changed. "Much prettier," said Gunda. "Get to know the real France," said Manfred. "Do what you like," said Leo, removing his earphones for the first time that day. But the alternative route didn't take account of weekend drivers, horses, and deaf and blind farmers who stubbornly gave way to no one.

Now, twenty-year-old camper van engines, unused for most of the year, often can't cope with the sudden task of driving 900 kms for fourteen hours on bumpy country roads, and this one was no exception. Gunda said at lunchtime that the smell of burning inside the vehicle wasn't right. Manfred said it was from bonfires and Leo said he was listening to Taylor Swift. By four o'clock, the smell was accompanied by a rather exciting noise when they accelerated. When they stopped at five-thirty, 250 kms from their destination, for a comfort break, both Manfred and Gunda thought the engine smelt hot and left the bonnet open for ten minutes. Leo took off his earphones for about thirty seconds, said he was hungry and put the earphones on again. At seven o'clock, when Gunda was driving, and at the entrance to Saint Florian, there was a small explosion from somewhere under her right foot. She slowed down. But when she tried to accelerate uphill to the town hall, the engine roared like a wounded elephant. *"Mein Gott!"* the couple said in unison. Leo thought it was the climax of the heavy metal track he was listening to and said, "Wow."

At the five little tables inside the *Café de la Poste*, Raimond was watching rugby with his friends, who met there every Saturday evening. Manfred spoke a little French but with a heavy German accent. *"Camionette kaput!"* he told a surprised Lucille behind the bar, who thought he was going to order at least three drinks. "Is there a garage in the village?"

Lucille said there was and nodded towards Raimond, who said with half a smile that unfortunately it wouldn't be open either on the Sunday or the Monday, which was May Day. He asked what the problem was. Manfred said there was a funny smell, then an explosion and then the van roared like this. And he made a startlingly loud 'vroom, vroom' noise so that it could be heard over the TV crowd noise, for Toulouse had scored another try. All the patrons first fell silent, then laughed, then went back to watching the match. Gunda and Leo looked embarrassed. Then, Gunda bent towards Raimond's ear and said in a tragic stage whisper, *"Ganz kaput,"* accompanied by a scissor-like gesture with both hands. Raimond rose slowly from his chair and put his cap on. Manfred thought that he saw him wink at the lady behind the bar.

From the bottom of the inspection pit in the garage, Raimond said that it was what he thought. He produced a bent piece of burnt rubber tube, which was split and still hot. He shook his head slowly and, pointing to the exhaust, said it would take a week to fix. He could make a temporary repair, but the vehicle fell into the vintage category and the spare part could only be found in Germany.

Raimond could see that the German family were tired and stressed. He suggested they stay the night at the village hotel. It was owned by his sister and the food was home-made. They could make their minds up during the weekend. Manfred told Gunda they had no choice. Gunda agreed but nevertheless asked Leo. He said he didn't know.

At breakfast, they were delighted to find four other couples from Holland, Denmark, England and Belgium. But they looked glum. By their second cup of excellent coffee, they had established that they had all followed the GPS alternative route; that they all had old cars; that none of them had serviced their vehicles before the trip and that they had all been told that their repairs would take a week. There was nothing to do in Saint Florian except sit in the spring sunshine, eat in the *Café de la Poste* and play *boules*. Leo met a sixteen-year-old French girl. They could not communicate but listened to music together. On the fifth day, when the van was fixed, they kissed.

Manfred reckoned the hotel made 1,000 euros a day from six rooms, twelve people, three meals a day, *tout compris.* No wonder Raimond winked.

THE PARROT

My friend, Kenneth, had a soft spot for animals. Anything wounded, starving or abandoned attracted him. He'd never married. Our office at Formans, the merchant bank, was often shared with a furry animal and a goldfish. He bought a rabbit at a farmer's market in Balham. It twitched in its hutch next to his desk. He said it had mental health issues. Kenneth used to kiss it on the nose. I found the performance repulsive.

But I admired the man because he really didn't care what anybody thought. His reaction to anything conventional was to challenge it. I was not surprised, for example, by his attitude to savings. He dismissed the idea that one shouldn't put all one's eggs in one basket. His other investment theory was that one should choose a small company in a growing market. He loved to tell me that for years he'd been buying shares in a small company making tennis shoes. It made tiny profits and declared meagre dividends. We used to tease him about his love affair with gym shoes. "Scoff if you like," he told me once, "but one day there'll be a boom in sneakers." ('Trainers' to you and I. He liked to use American words.)

Then, about two years ago, Kenneth caught Covid. I thought he'd shaken it off but his behaviour changed. He started making errors. He had headaches all the time, seemed permanently fatigued and had what he called 'brain fog'. I now think it was all invented. He started holding phone calls in the corridor. When he was out, which was often, I took messages for him and most of them were from a big American athletic footwear company.

He left the bank quite suddenly last autumn. Before I'd had a chance to organise farewell drinks for him, he'd cleared his desk, disposed of his rabbit and goldfish, and was gone. I tried to contact him by phone but the number no longer worked. So, I gave up.

Imagine my surprise when, six months later, Alice and I were invited to dinner chez Kenneth in South Kensington. Another couple, Mark and Joanna, arrived at the same time. Joanna is in accounts at Formans and Mark is an insurance broker. Like us, they had guessed it was a sort of housewarming party and had brought an ornamental ivy plant in a fancy pot. We brought an imitation crystal ball and a bottle of prosecco. The front door just needed pushing to open.

We didn't see our host at first but assumed the trainers poking from under the table were his. The legs jerked and I wondered whether poor Kenneth was having a fit. Having carefully saved the rather chic bag holding my prosecco for use another time, I bent down and lifted the tablecloth. Kenneth had his arms around something large, covered by a green bath towel.

"So sorry. Blasted parrot. African Grey. Great disappointment. Bought it two years ago from a lovely couple – genuine cockneys. They told me it talked but it hasn't said a word. Meant to answer to the name of George. Have to keep him in his cage when anyone else is in the house. Gets jealous and squawks. Only way to catch a parrot is with a towel."

George was tipped into his cage, then he blinked in the way that parrots do and ate a Brazil nut. Kenneth then gave us a short guided tour. The flat was luxurious and futuristic. The lights dimmed or brightened on voice command; a bookcase pivoted to turn into a bar; another bookcase slid open to reveal an electronic keyboard. There was a round yellow-marble coffee table that turned silently on ball bearings, and a softly lit display of Lalique crystal sculptures. A state-of-the-art entertainment system, a smart wardrobe in the bedroom and a glass hydroponic cupboard in the kitchen for growing vegetables all year round.

I'd worked with Kenneth for the best part of ten years. Our salaries were identical. Alice and I had been to his old flat in Tooting several times and it was modest, comfortable and a bit old-fashioned, just like ours. So, I knew there was no way he could have afforded a place like this normally. I was dying to know how he'd done it but thought it rude to ask outright.

The conversation started predictably with the usual local gossip – the latest rail strikes; the police failing to catch car thieves; trying to get a doctor's appointment. We couldn't believe it when, at the words "doctor's appointment", the parrot rocked back and forth and started laughing.

With the prosecco long finished, Kenneth retired to prepare dinner behind yet another sliding screen. As he switched on his food processor, all the lights went out. We heard a very rude word, presumably from Kenneth, and Mark lit some scented candles. Kenneth fiddled with the fuse box to no avail. Jo and Alice said it would be romantic with candles. All I could think to say was that candles reminded me of my old aunt's funeral the week before. She lived alone in Vauxhall Bridge Road and collected plastic bags in case they came in useful. They were floor-to-ceiling and she couldn't get to the phone to call an ambulance after she'd had a stroke. We all agreed that '*might come in useful one day*' should have been written on her gravestone.

Because Kenneth now had to change the menu from hot to cold, we all drank a bit too much wine, including our host. I felt bold enough by the dessert and cheese to ask whether he missed the bank and why he left so suddenly.

He paused, swirling wine round his glass. "A misunderstanding with the partners," he said. "I was handling the American athletic footwear account. They made a brilliant acquisition of this little tennis shoe company in the UK."

"Yes. The one in Birmingham? The one you told me about so often?"

"That's right." Kenneth paused again. "Turned out that I had become a significant shareholder one way and another. So, when the Americans acquired it, I was sitting pretty."

There was complete silence around the table. Wallace was admitting to blatant insider trading, admitting to a massive criminal offence. He produced a decanter of port and begged us to taste it because it was special.

"When the partners at Formans found out, they panicked and sacked me on the spot. I told them how delighted the American company was; that I had worked on this account for the best part of a year; that Formans had earned more fees with this one deal than they had in the six previous months; and that their accusations of insider trading were unjustified. The fact that I had been investing myself in the British company for many years – via a third party, of course – didn't affect the deal. As partners, they were as implicated as much as I was."

My heart started racing as it all sank in. Alice looked at her watch. Joanna looked open-mouthed at Mark. We all felt very uneasy.

"I don't feel the slightest bit guilty," Kenneth said.

"Porky pies. Porky pies," the parrot squawked.

Kenneth got up and put a cloth over his cage.

"What did he say?" Alice whispered to me.

"It's cockney rhyming slang for 'lies'," I whispered back.

"Won't you have some coffee?" Kenneth said. There were no takers.

Three minutes later, we all left the flat.

ALL SAINTS' DAY

It's rather sad that religious festivals have become so commercialised and stripped of their original meaning. Easter is now about chocolate eggs and bunnies. Christmas is about sales and presents. Halloween is about witches and devils, and it overshadows All Saints' Day in church and the 2nd of November in cemeteries where the faithful remember dead relatives and friends. There's a practical aspect to the cemetery visit in France. Families themselves are responsible for maintaining family graves. The florists do good business selling chrysanthemums. In Mexico, on the *Día de los Muertos,* the dead are believed to return to earth and are invited to graveside family picnics. All Saints' Day in France also coincides with the half-term holiday. This is when William and Isabella Kemp always closed their old farmhouse for the winter.

Their village in rural France, like thousands of others, is redolent with history. King François I, in 1515 or thereabouts, became lost and separated from his courtiers whilst hunting on horseback in the surrounding hills. He was grudgingly accommodated for the night, and fed by one of the locals in the village, who only discovered the identity of his guest the next day when the courtiers came looking for him.

It's difficult to imagine how tough and dangerous life must have been for those peasant farmers five hundred years ago. Finding food to put on the table took up most of their time. Part of whatever meagre crops they grew had to be given as tithes to the *seigneur* in his castle five miles away. And there were brigands who made their living by robbing the peasants. The Kemp's farmhouse was a bit like a fortress on the side of a steep hill. It was protected by very high stone walls, with arrow slits on either side of the massive wooden entrance gate. The two other farmhouses on the lower side of the lane were similarly protected.

During the chaos of the Revolution and the Reign of Terror that followed, people hid or buried their valuables wherever they could. One such hiding place was discovered, with contents, in one of the houses at the top of the village. All the Kemps found at their house, however, was a three-hundred-year-old silver coin in their courtyard.

The All Saints' holiday last year started with some excitement. As the Kemps approached their house, they saw with alarm a police van, two *gendarmes* – one young, one old – and their French neighbour and true friend, Edouard Perrault. The place where they usually parked, between their barn and the lane, had been taped off by the police. Their massive two-metre-high wooden gate was open and Edouard had the key in his hand. He'd used it the week before when the chimney sweep came. William parked behind the police van with his heart pounding.

Was this a burglary? If so, the burglars had chosen a good moment when most of the houses were empty at a holiday weekend. Once Edouard had introduced the Kemps to the *gendarmes* and they were satisfied as to their identities, they all moved indoors. Isabella wondered whether to offer them some suitable refreshment but then thought better of it. The inevitable notebooks were produced whilst the Kemps made a quick inspection of the house. Surprisingly, nothing was missing. They kept little of real value there anyway. The two, enormous seventeenth-century wardrobes were still there and hadn't been unlocked as far as they could tell.

"We've been here since eight this morning," said the older *gendarme,* a warrant officer. "And Monsieur Perrault has been most helpful. He saw a car's lights outside this house at about three this morning."

Edouard nodded in agreement. "I'm sorry that I didn't come down straight away to investigate though. I thought it was either a hunter or a couple of lovers. Both like to park here. It's dark and secluded."

The Kemps still didn't know what had happened. Consulting his notebook, the older *gendarme* told them. "Between midnight and three am, a male, working alone, scaled your perimeter wall with a ladder and jumped down the other side. He made a mess of your flower-pots, I'm afraid. He then went straight to your basement and cut the rusty chain on the door down there. We've left it where it was, in case forensics want to look at it. We've photographed various tyre tracks and footprints."

"But why on earth," said my wife, "did he want to go down to the cellar to begin with? It's not the sort of place a burglar goes to first, is it?"

"For *this*, Madame," said the older *gendarme* as he bent sideways to take from his pocket a clear plastic bag, which he put on the table. It contained a rather stiff and dirty leather pouch with a drawstring. It was the size of a small shoe.

"He knew what he was doing, what he was looking for and where to look. In the wall, opposite the old bread oven, there's a small recess. It was there."

All the farmhouses had stone-built, wood-fired bread ovens. The Kemps' oven was in their cellar. Each farmer's wife took it in turns to bake once a week, sharing the bread with their neighbours.

"I'm amazed we didn't find it ourselves," Isabella said.

"The good news is he's under arrest already. He was asleep in the room the commune had given him when he was released from prison. It's a sad case. A petty thief who seemed to do well in the Foreign Legion. He was dismissed for theft after five years. No family. No funds. More crime, despite our keeping an eye on him."

The sub-lieutenant now took over. "He left this behind in the pouch. A gold coin. He's refusing to say what he's done with the rest of the treasure. Says he's never been to this hamlet, doesn't know where it is and has no car. But he might talk when he's been with us a bit longer."

"I'm pretty sure," said the older *gendarme,* "that he's already passed on what he found to whoever's paying him. We'd like to know the identity of that person. It's someone with an intimate knowledge of your house."

The Kemps looked at each other. Isabella shivered. William pursed his lips.

Edouard had been silent but now said, "A local wouldn't dare."

"Do you have any idea who it might be, Madame?"

"No. But we would dearly like to know," Isabella said.

"After an incident like this, people will start chattering in the café and rumours will fly around. We'll keep our ears open," said the *gendarme*.

"Anyway, we always go to mass on All Saints' Day and then on to the cemetery," said the older *gendarme*.

"For the gossip," said the younger one. His colleague stared at him disapprovingly.

"Intelligence, not gossip," he said, standing up. They readjusted the pistols at their belts and picked up their phones and notebooks. He looked at Edouard and said, "Any ideas?"

"One has one's suspicions," Edouard said. "I'll say no more," and he left, too.

COFFEE WITH OLEG

O ne of the interesting things about London is the way communities from overseas have chosen to settle in unlikely spots. Portuguese in Vauxhall, Koreans in New Malden, Japanese in Finchley, Ethiopians in Battersea and so on. These communities are often centred round particular schools or religious centres. Famously, the French favoured South Kensington or adjacent boroughs, close to their *lycée*, cultural centres and consulate. For many years after the war, they shared South Kensington with another large expatriate community – the Poles. From 1939 onwards, thousands of Polish exiles lived close to their clubs, community centre and exiled government. But after the war, the area gradually became too expensive and many moved south to Balham.

David Mason, fifty-two, had become part of the Russian and Eastern European community in London ever since he returned from his two years of postgraduate studies in Kraków. He was a gifted linguist. It was the challenge the Slavic languages represented that attracted him more than anything else. He was a rare bird; an Englishman who spoke

Polish, Russian and Czech fluently. He taught for five years at the Department of Slavic Languages and Literatures at Harvard before coming back as a professor at the School of Slavonic and East European Studies in London.

David's family was as thoroughly English as could be. Many of his ancestors – doctors, priests and lawyers, for the most part – came from a small village on the Hampshire/Berkshire border. The village was known for two things. In the round barrows among the surrounding stunningly beautiful hills, archaeologists discovered traces of a civilisation that came to be known as the 'Beaker People', because the men and women inside those tombs were found with beakers beside them. For an afterlife, perhaps?

The other, much more gruesome sight, was a gibbet. It had been there (with seven replacements) since 1676 when the bodies of two murderers, a man and a woman, were hung there. They had been having an adulterous affair and were caught *in flagrante delicto* by the man's wife and son. They were tried, found guilty and executed in Winchester, and their bodies hung on the gibbet as a warning to others.

We digress. David Mason's career in London was a success story. As an independent academic, he was one of the few 'go-to' people for comments in the media about Russian and Eastern European affairs. Despite being scrupulously objective, the regimes he studied decided that he was unfriendly. He accumulated a wealth of information about corruption and criminality in Russia. He wrote a bestseller. He found himself a minor celebrity.

Making good use of his network of good friends in Eastern Europe and Russia, David launched an initially successful podcast. But then things took an ominous turn.

After only six months, it suffered from repeated technical glitches. Worse still, people who downloaded it imported a bug onto their own devices. He had to abandon podcasting.

His house was burgled while he and his wife were abroad. They couldn't see that anything was stolen but they both saw it as a warning that he had upset powerful people. Worst of all, he received death threats on social media. No reason was given. He told the police, of course. But David accepted that this sort of thing was to be expected. It went with the territory. He put it to the back of his mind.

One Saturday morning in May last year, as he walked down Balham High Road, David marvelled at how profoundly the place had changed. Gone were the hardware shops catering to young couples doing up their own houses. Gone were the second-hand furniture shops. Gone were the bank branches, the newsagents, the betting shops, the doner kebabs and Chinese takeaways. Even the post office had downsized. In their place, there were chichi restaurants, electric bicycle shops, nail salons and expensive hairdressers. Best of all, there was a new bookshop and coffee bar.

The owner of the bookshop was young, charismatic and keen. He readily agreed to David doing a wine-and-cheese book signing. And because the shop was not too far from the Polish club and church, David would often bump into people he knew. More people were out on Saturdays partly because of the farmer's market nearby. The High Road was buzzing on that sunny Saturday and David found the bookshop door wedged open to let in the fresh air.

The sequence of events thereafter remained etched on his mind, not least because he had to repeat them many times to the police. He chose a paperback *(Travels with a donkey in the Cévennes)* after just a couple of minutes. He then chatted to the bookshop owner about his own book ("Selling like hot cakes," he said) and paid for the paperback and a cappuccino. To his delight, he recognised an old Russian writer friend, Oleg Petrov, sitting with a tea and with his back to the shelf holding the sugar, napkins and so on. He had just published an excellent, honest book about contemporary Russia. David greeted him warmly and sat opposite him at the small round table in the front of the shop. They talked in Russian.

On the pavement outside, David noticed a youngish man with unusually jet-black hair and wearing sunglasses, ostensibly looking at the books in the window, but glancing for several seconds at a time at Oleg and David. He was accompanied by a woman with perfectly groomed auburn hair, also wearing sunglasses. They came into the shop but didn't return the owner's 'good morning', which was a bit unusual. The man went straight to the counter and asked for two double espressos. As they were being prepared, the woman seemed to be choosing a book from the beautifully arranged tables that held the bestsellers and the owner's picks of the week. Several times, she looked towards her man friend. Then, there was an almighty crash as she knocked over two piles of books onto the floor. The man with black hair had moved behind Oleg to pick up some sugar and two stirrers. Oleg had turned sideways to see what was happening. But David, for some lucky reason, kept his eyes on Oleg. He saw the man with black hair fumbling with a miniature whisky bottle and then stumbling over David and Oleg's table while all eyes were on what was happening at the back of the shop.

David shouted at Oleg not to touch his tea or anything on their table. Before either of them could get up, the couple in sunglasses had left the shop and were running down the High Road.

The bookshop owner was the very model of calm and quick thinking. In his previous life, he had been a respected journalist. After two words with David, he phoned 999 and – to the distress of the half dozen other clients in the shop – locked the door until armed counter-terrorism police arrived.

It was later that night that the police spokesman at Scotland Yard confirmed that there had been an unsuccessful attempt to kill Oleg Petrov in Balham. He also confirmed that a man and a woman, both thought to be Russian, had been found by a cleaner in toilets at Heathrow Airport's Terminal 4. They were wearing wigs and were clutching miniature whisky bottles. They were dead. Later, forensic tests showed they had been poisoned.

IS ANGELA THERE?

Anne had long maintained that women could feel things and could sense things that men couldn't. Her husband, Gordon, agreed. He used to joke about his paranormal wife but stopped when Anne told him that it was no longer funny. Anne could sense marital problems before a couple could articulate them; could sense the tension of a taxi driver in a traffic jam. She could sense when the weather was going to change. Intuition is what made her an outstanding nurse and, later, a brilliant hospital matron. Walking into a hospital ward, she knew within seconds whether it was running well or badly. She knew when a patient was in pain before the doctors did.

Since retirement, one of her joys was her grandchildren. One of them, fifteen-year-old Patricia, was at boarding school in Dorset. She was to spend Boat Race weekend in London with Anne and Gordon. Both had rowed at university and relived their rowing days on Boat Race Day each year.

Thinking of her safety, travelling alone, Patricia's parents had booked their daughter a first-class return to

London, which cost an arm and a leg. Quite an experienced traveller, Patricia had done this journey twice before. The train was due to arrive at six-thirty. Just as Anne was about to leave the house to go to the station to meet her, her mobile rang.

"Hi, it's me." Patricia never called Anne 'Granny', so the greeting was normal.

"Hello, darling. I'm about to catch the bus to meet you at the station, as agreed."

"Is Angela there?" asked Patricia. "Angela," she said again.

Anne was puzzled. She did not know anyone called Angela. "I'm sorry, you must have the wrong number," she said.

"Angela, yes?" said the voice again. Then the line went dead.

As she put her mobile back in her pocket, Anne's sixth sense told her that something was not right. It had sounded like Patricia's voice, yet the tone was higher. She set off in good time for the bus stop. There was normally a bus to the station every ten minutes. Fifteen minutes passed, then twenty – no bus arrived. She looked anxiously up and down the road for a black cab. No black cab in sight. By now, it was six-twenty and she was ever-so-slightly panicking. To her relief, a white saloon car stopped, the window opened and the youngish lady driver asked if she could give Anne a lift.

"That's incredibly kind. Yes please. I'm going to the station and I'm late."

"No problem. Hop in. It's on my way."

The car smelt of lavender and leather.

"Sling my handbag onto the back seat. You travelling far?"

"Actually, I'm meeting my granddaughter. Boat Race weekend. She's only fifteen. She's coming up from school in Dorset."

"Train's bound to be late," the lady said.

"I think she phoned from the train just now, but we were cut off and she didn't phone back. But I'm now wondering whether it was a wrong number. The person was asking for Angela and I…"

"Oh my God!" said the driver. "Angela! Angela is the code word to use when you feel unsafe. In a pub, if you ask the staff for Angela, they'll ask you if you need some help with a difficult man. If you feel unsafe or threatened, you know?"

"No, I didn't know. Never heard about it. This is awful."

The lady miraculously found a parking place on the station forecourt. The two of them then ran to the platform as the train was being announced. Anne looked to see if there was a railway official on the platform, but there was none. They guessed rightly that the first-class carriage was at the front of the train. Patricia was the first out of the carriage – book and phone in one hand, backpack in the other. Typically, even though it was April, she was wearing midsummer clothes. She was not followed and Anne couldn't see any more than the shadow of a man inside the carriage before it left for Waterloo.

"My job's done," my friend said. "I'll leave you two together."

Anne thanked her profusely. She disappeared into the crowd as the rain started.

In the taxi going to her grandparent's house, Patricia was pale, shivering and unusually silent. She had, by now, fished a crumpled coat out of her bag and put it on. All she said in the taxi was "Did you get my call?", before saying they would talk later.

Once back at the house, as she was washing her hands upstairs, Anne said to Gordon, "I'm sure there's been an incident on the train. I don't know what it was. Poor Patricia has been shaken by something."

A little while later, sitting on a stool in the kitchen as Anne prepared supper, Patricia started talking about it. "There were only four people in the compartment when I got on at Sherbourne. I thought I would be safe sitting opposite the oldest one. He was as old as you," Patricia said, looking at Gordon. They laughed. "But it was a bad choice," she continued. "He started by asking if I was interested in dinosaurs. I said, 'Sort of.' He said he used to do programmes for TV. He said could he show me a painting he'd done – I think he said of a pliosaur. Some name like that. It was on his phone. He got up and sat next to me, scrolling through weird stuff."

"What sort of weird stuff?" Gordon asked.

"Well, one was a selfie of the old man made up as a clown. Another was a clip of him playing nursery rhymes on a flute and kids dancing and singing."

Gordon and Anne looked at each other without speaking.

Patricia continued, "His painting was very realistic. He said it was based on a colossal skull that had been found on the cliffs in Dorset. He said it was the most fearsome predator the planet had ever seen. I said, 'Wow, that's amazing,' and I opened my book as if to finish the conversation. But he then put his hand on my knee and said he had more to show me. By this time, I was becoming scared. I said I had to make a phone call and I called you. He went back to his seat opposite me but was listening and smiling at me in a funny way."

Anne and Gordon still took a newspaper on Saturdays. Patricia was leafing through it when she spotted a photo of the old man in the train under the headline: *Dinosaur Man in Frame to Be Head of Children's TV.*

In the end, Gordon only watched the first few minutes of the Boat Race. Cambridge won yet again. The rest of the weekend he spent on the phone warning everyone he could think of about Dinosaur Man. He needn't have bothered really because the old man died under a cliff fall in Dorset a fortnight later.

FULL CIRCLE

The view over Florence from the boutique hotel's garden in Bellosguardo was more than just picturesque. There was something timeless, almost holy, about it. Like an opera set – blue hills in the distance, terracotta roof tiles atop sixteenth-century *palazzi* in the centre and vertical green/black cypresses providing the foreground frame. Angela Reef, thirty-two last week, had arrived with her twelve-year-old son, David, from London an hour earlier. She was already sitting with a Campari Soda on the terrace watching the September sun set. David had a juice with ice cubes and a straw. They were floating in the warm air, lulled by the scent of lavender bushes abuzz with battalions of bees.

The trip to Florence was disguised as a birthday present to herself. Angela hadn't been back there since she was twenty. She had agonised for months and months about the wisdom of returning. Was it worth the risk? She had been so blissfully happy, learning Italian at the British Institute and sketching, that she feared that revisiting her old haunts would be a disappointment. But, of course, above all, there was a personal reason for coming. She had some unfinished business. It was a huge gamble.

She had been swept off her feet all those years ago by Giovanni, who was using the Institute's magnificent library for research for his thesis on map-making in the Renaissance. Angela was using the library for her homework. It had started with what was meant to be a quick lunch, which, in fact, lasted until early evening. With Giovanni, life in Florence took on another dimension. He delayed telling her where he lived with his parents until she was head-over-heels in love with him and he with her. Only then did he reveal what she had already suspected – that his family was one of the oldest in Florence and that its preservation was an unspoken priority. He would inherit the title of *barone*. They were not badly matched because Angela's family, too, could trace its roots clearly back to the fourteenth century and there was a family manor house in Northumberland.

Giovanni introduced her slowly to his world. Many of the old Florentine families still held a special place in local affairs. They were tolerated, even respected, as long as they maintained their historic buildings, their art collections and their country estates. They had to keep a low profile and not seek to impose themselves. Some of the noble families with vineyards had increased their fortunes considerably. Some had made money out of tourism. But some struggled to maintain standards, to live as their parents did. Their high-ceilinged, musty Renaissance houses always seemed cold. Their antique furniture needed repairing and their pictures restoring. The families trusted Giovanni to study the maps in their libraries. He took Angela with him. She was amazed to find these elderly Florentines spoke the most beautiful English. They said it had been learned from their English nannies.

The English colony in Tuscany, at the time Angela was there, was a sad reflection of what it had once been. It was an eccentric relic of a bygone age. She remembered they gathered for weekly lectures, tea or bridge parties. The ladies dressed in chiffon and eau de cologne. The men wore off-white, stained linen jackets with coloured pocket handkerchiefs. Their accents hadn't changed since Noel Coward's time. Florence had always attracted English outsiders and Angela met some of them at a reception given by the British Consul. It was a relief after that party to fall into the arms of someone normal – Giovanni. Her Italian improved no end with Giovanni's tuition. Angela was renting a tiny top-floor flat near the Porta Romana. They would cook pasta with outrageous sauces and crunchy salads; drink good Chianti and make love. Angela hoped that by some miracle he would ask her to marry him, but in her heart of hearts she knew he would not. They were both too young.

Their last evening together was tearful and tumultuous and full of love. Their last kiss was on the Ponte Santa Trinita. Angela had a scholarship to the Slade School of Fine Art, starting when she left Florence, and it would have been madness not to take it up. Giovanni was expected to take over a large family antiques business once he had his doctorate. So, against all their emotional instincts, they had solemnly agreed not to see each other again. It was a bitterly cruel decision. They knew they would live to regret it. But they both kept their word.

Twelve years later, life looked very different for both of them. After returning from Florence, Angela had given birth to David. There was no doubt that Giovanni was the father. With her parents' understanding and practical help, David had been brought up better than most single-parent children. He'd inherited his mother's talents for languages (Italian, fluently) and drawing. David had often asked who his father was. She had managed to satisfy his curiosity by talking about fictional, anonymous indiscretions while she was in Italy – how she had been silly; how there was no way of knowing. But she could not maintain the pretence once David's grandmother had let the cat out of the bag. Angela had asked David whether he was ready to meet his father. David had said he was more than ready; he was longing to do so.

Angela had found Giovanni's contact details on his business website. She debated as to whether she should phone or write. Telling Giovanni on the phone that he had a son in England would have been a massive shock. She decided to write. It had been the most difficult message she had ever written in her life. She attached a photo of herself and David.

Giovanni's reaction, whilst cautious, had been surprisingly positive. He said every single detail of their time together was indelibly etched on his memory. He frequently dreamt of Angela. He still had the rose she had given him on their last night together. Yes, they should certainly meet. No, he was not married any longer. It was a sad story; his wife couldn't have children but it took a long time to find out.

They arranged to meet at the Neptune Fountain in the Boboli Gardens in the middle of the morning. Angela thought David would enjoy the challenge of sketching in the Boboli while she kept him in her line of sight and talked to Giovanni.

Angela recognised Giovanni immediately as he strode towards the fountain purposefully. His hair was slightly grey at the edges. There were suggestions of wrinkles on his forehead but his smile hadn't changed a bit. They embraced for a long moment. David saw everything – the look of happiness on his mother's face above all.

"Shorter hair really suits you. I somehow knew we would be together again. I thought it would be sooner than this," Giovanni said before David had joined them.

"Better late than never," said Angela, rather lamely. "This is David."

"He's much taller than I expected. Hello. I'm Giovanni, an old friend of your mother."

David smiled, then said in perfect Italian, "Don't let's play games. I know exactly who you are. And I'm really, truly happy to meet you."

Giovanni, for once, was lost for words. But his smile spoke volumes. He put a protective fatherly arm across David's shoulders and suggested the three of them go for lunch on the other side of the river. His arm rested on David's shoulder the whole way.

MOBILE PHONES

It was about two in the afternoon and the tube was baking hot. June was breaking temperature records once more. The air coming into the carriage was stale and dusty like the air from my vacuum cleaner. There were never many passengers going south of the river at this time of day. I often tried to guess from their clothes who they were. Most had their eyes fixed on their phones. The man fast asleep, with his head on the partition glass by the door, was surely an off-duty tube driver going home. Two older men with white Panama hats were probably going to watch the afternoon's cricket at the Oval. The lady staring into space and listening intently to something with her big black earphones looked like a singer on her way to a rehearsal.

Then, I noticed the woman sitting opposite me. She was clutching a plastic shopping-bag as if it were going to run away. Her other hand was making a fist while she looked every few moments at the map of the Northern Line above where I was sitting. She was tense and perspiring. I guessed rightly that she was a nurse – sensible shoes, short hair, no make-up. I looked away for a few minutes but could sense she was troubled. Two stations before mine at Clapham South, she reached into her bag and I could see a name tag on her uniform with *Guy's Hospital Staff Nurse Sandra* on it.

"I see you're at Guy's. I've just come from there – the Cancer Centre."

She looked at me, surprised. She had to be suspicious of a much older man trying to chat her up.

"Second session of chemo," I added, pointing to the wash-proof plaster on my arm.

"That's where I work," she said. She had a slight Scottish accent. She had auburn hair and freckles.

"In the Cancer Centre?" I asked. She nodded. "What a coincidence," I said.

As Clapham South approached, I stood up to leave and so did she. She was agitated and her eyes had narrowed.

"Are you alright?" I said, feeling slightly foolish as our feet touched the platform.

"I'll be fine," she said as we walked. The train rattled off towards Balham. To my huge surprise, she added, "You shouldn't be walking around in this heat immediately after chemotherapy. There should be someone with you and you need to take it easy for the rest of the day."

"I know. That's true. We both need hydrating – at least I do," I said on the escalator. We agreed to stop at the little coffee place at the station exit.

Even while drinking her mineral water, her hand was shaking and her speech was a bit disjointed. It turned out that she'd had her phone stolen outside the hospital during her lunch break. She'd been meeting her sister who worked at London Bridge Hospital. To eat their sandwiches, they'd squeezed onto a seat around a big plane tree in the little garden opposite the medical school. It was a popular spot in the shade. Her phone was in her shopping bag beside her. She was conscious of a tall young man with curly fair hair wearing a Taylor Swift T-shirt beside the bag. She took him to be a medical student. When he left after a couple of minutes, his place was immediately taken by another student, tapping on her phone at incredible speed. Only when Sandra had finished her sandwich and when her sister had stopped talking, did she realise her phone had gone.

"I couldn't believe it. It's not what you'd expect there, is it? I had a sort of panic attack. I scanned all the people sitting nearby to see if the young man was there. Nowhere to be seen, of course." She paused. "But the good news is *this*." She pulled a phone out of her bag and lowered her voice to a whisper. "It's my sister's and I've got to give it back to her tonight." She pointed to the mapping app. "My sister and I can track each other. By one-thirty, I could see my phone was on the corner here." She pointed to the middle of the screen. "I was determined to find it. My sister had to go back to work. See, the phone's location hasn't moved."

I knew exactly where it was on the map. A lot flashed through my mind. Had the phone been thrown away? Should we call the police? What if the thief had a knife? Was I strong enough to help if it came to a fight?

"It's in Nightingale Lane, a couple of minutes from here. It's on my way home," I said. "I'll come with you. You shouldn't tackle him alone."

We both finished our water.

"I'm desperate to get it back," she said. "I can't live without it. My duty roster's on there. My Uber app. My bank stuff. All my messages. My photos. My life, really. I'm prepared to risk anything."

We both saw the tall youth in the Taylor Swift T-shirt at the same time. He was sitting on a bench in front of a block of flats.

"Excuse me, but that's my phone you're looking at," Sandra said, standing in front of him. Caught completely by surprise, the youth looked at her open-mouthed. I drew myself up to my full height – six-foot three – and took a step towards him.

"I found it," he said, "over there, by the tennis courts."

"No, you didn't. You took it from my shopping bag outside Guy's Hospital at lunchtime, didn't you?"

"You can't prove it," he said, raising his voice, thinking he'd scored a point. He had a middle-class, even posh, accent.

"Well, I can prove it's mine," Sandra said. "This gentleman with me will make it ring from his phone when I give him the number."

So, I was now fully involved. I saw he was much younger than I had first thought. "How old are you?" I asked.

"Fifteen," he replied.

"You should know better," I said. "Why did you steal it?"

He paused. "I used to have one," he said. "Since I was eleven, I've had one. But a month ago, my parents took it off me, locked it up somewhere, while I was doing my GCSE's. Now the exams are finished, I asked for it back, but my dad said he'll only give it back when I'm sixteen. That's six months from now. He's cruel." His eyes filled with tears and he looked scared. "I've got no life without a phone. I need to text my friends every day. Chat with them. Find out where they are, what they're doing. I need my music. I need to see my girlfriend. Can't keep in touch with her without a phone. Do you know what I mean?"

He looked lost and rather sad. He handed the phone back to Sandra.

"What can I do?" he asked me. There was another pause.

"Wait till you're sixteen," I said.

COMRADE GRAVAK

Comrade Gravak, a lifelong fifty-year-old bachelor with bad teeth, had been allocated the best ground-floor flat in the block at 55 Lublin Street, Warsaw. It was beside the lift, with sole access to the garden. Not that he grew anything in the garden. He only used it to dry his washing. All the other residents thought he was a pain in the neck, and dangerous. He saw who was coming in, who was going out, with what shopping and how many visitors they had.

Irina and Anna Komar had been allocated a two-room flat on the fourth floor and had been there for ten years. One of the few pleasures they had was to annoy Comrade Gravak whenever they could. Other residents did the same but were less inventive. For the Komar sisters, irritating the comrade, who was a paid informer, had become something of a fine art.

Living in communist Poland in the late 1960s was a struggle from morning until night. Irina liked to compare her life to that of a wasp. Her beloved country had become a wasp's nest. The pretence was that it was a successful collective effort but actually it was every wasp for itself. They followed each other around blindly and if they chose to fight, they probably died. Not much of a life.

Some of the sadness was because both Irina and Anna were already widows. Irina's husband had been murdered by the Russians – part of the mass executions carried out by the NKVD on Stalin's orders in April and May 1940, mostly in the forests at Katyn. "Imagine," she would say, "just imagine: twenty-two thousand men massacred in that forest in two months." Anna's husband, who had been in the Resistance, had been killed by the Germans on the other side of Poland, in Poznan, in 1944. "We Poles were unlucky with our wartime neighbours," she used to say, with that black humour of hers.

It was a forty-five-minute journey for Irina from the flat to the Veteran's Office where she worked in the centre of Warsaw. If the lift was working, if the snow had been cleared and if she could push her way onto the tram, the journey time was five minutes less. Sometimes, she couldn't resist an early morning treat: emptying her mailbox of Communist party rubbish and putting it in Comrade Gravak's mailbox. Twenty second's work; one hundred per cent satisfaction. Big wars were won, Irina told Anna, by winning small battles.

Irina was lucky to have been given the Veteran's Office job. It was no doubt because her husband was a Katyn Forest victim. She was in the Vouchers and Discounts Team and was often offered bribes, mostly from men wanting to be on the veteran's gravy train. She had been accepting these 'gifts' for years. The actual exchange of extra vouchers for a 'present' usually took place in the weekly market in the Old

Town, where it didn't look suspicious to be seen carrying strange things in sacks – rabbits, musical instruments, spare parts for Trabant cars. Her best 'present', just before Christmas, was from an alcoholic veteran who spent his pension on vodka. He gave her a dozen freshwater crayfish, undoubtedly stolen from the state, in return for a dozen vouchers, also stolen from the state. The live crayfish came in an old bucket and made a lot of scratching noises. The tram ride to the flat was stressful enough. But, as bad luck would have it, one of the crayfish had managed to get its front claws over the edge of the bucket when Irina arrived back at her block of flats. Comrade Gravak spotted it and, on Christmas Day, two policemen arrived. They left twenty minutes later after a vodka each and two crayfish.

Anna's contribution to the cost of living was food. She worked in the local hospital kitchen as an assistant cook. She had perfected some foolproof schemes in conjunction with the nursing staff in palliative care on the top floor. Scheme One – after a death, they would delay notifying the kitchen of one less meal to prepare for a couple of vital hours so that Anna could put the unwanted meal into a large gherkin jar and smuggle it home. Scheme Two – the folk who were dying on the top floor often didn't eat their meals, so Anna did. Scheme Three – to avoid wasting leftovers, Anna put them in a specially adapted handbag so that Comrade Gravak wouldn't notice.

The Polish United Worker's Party held its annual Congress in Warsaw in early November, often coinciding with the first snowfall. Comrade Gravak couldn't resist telling everyone from June onwards that he had been invited to the Congress. For him, it was the pinnacle of his party career; a long-awaited recognition of his loyalty; a transcending honour. He was to be an usher.

The Congress was always held in the hideous socialist-realist Palace of Culture, built in 1955. At the time, it was the tallest skyscraper in Europe. A gift from Stalin, it was completed in three years by 3,500 builders imported directly from the Soviet Union. Poles hated it, both aesthetically and for the communism it stood for. But there was no denying that its facilities as a home for the performing arts were first-class. It was for Poland what the South Bank in London was to the UK – a centre of excellence. The Palace, with its red-plush seats, held 3,000 people.

So many basic things, not to mention luxuries like bananas, were in short supply, were rationed or were for the privileged. Queueing was a part of daily life. Even twenty years after the war was over, it was difficult to find decent meat or self-raising flour or caster sugar or white paint or jeans. If Irena or Anna saw a queue, they joined it and only asked what it was for later. Besides, queues were useful for catching up on what was really going on in the world. It was in one such queue, for East German washing-up liquid, that Irina had her best idea yet when the queue-talk turned to carrier pigeons.

It was Anna that had to provide the vital ingredient for the ruse – sunflowers from church. One of the curiosities of those communist times in post-war Poland was that the Catholic Church was allowed to continue as it always had. The Poles were as devout as the Irish, perhaps more so, because in church they could chat, keep up with the rumours, spread new ones and pray for a return to the old days. The faithful could also help by disposing of the dead flowers from the church. A week before Congress, Anna returned to the flat with an enormous bunch of wilting sunflowers. Comrade Gravak saw her but his mind was on higher things. If people wanted sunflowers to decorate their rooms, he wasn't going to stop them.

Now, there was no shortage of pigeons in Warsaw. When times were really bad, people caught and ate them. To summon the birds to 55 Lublin Street was easy. The sisters had a tiny but invaluable balcony overlooking the garden. Every square centimetre of it was used for storing or growing food, for keeping boots and jam jars and things-that-might-come-in-useful-one-day. This was where they put out the four bowls of sunflower seeds and saw, in the garden below, that Comrade Gravak had hung out the white shirt and beige trousers that he would wear for the Congress next day.

The pigeons weren't slow to arrive. Dozens of them jostled, cooed and fluttered around the bowls. This was manna from heaven. They lined up on the balcony railing and did what pigeons do, onto the drying washing below. Irina and Anna refilled the bowls three times and couldn't stop giggling.

Showing the party faithful to their seats next morning, Comrade Gravak's clothes were stained by pigeon excreta. He looked like a scarecrow. The superintendent of ushers told him so and sent him home.

"We shall *never* surrender," Anna said in English, mimicking Churchill.

THE STUDIO

S ophie Tervil had chosen to live in Shoreham-by-Sea partly because her late husband remembered it fondly from his school days at Lancing College and partly because she had a passion for sea swimming, which was good there. The steep pebble beach was ideal and there were no currents. There was something about the light that made it special for serious artists like herself. But in the twenty years she had lived there, the town had grown and changed. Shopping used to be such a pleasure; shop staff used to know her and were chatty. It was so different these days. Now, she regularly did her supermarket shopping without talking to a soul – unless she bought a bottle of gin and a bored staff member had to verify she was over eighteen before she could put it in her basket.

The supermarket was really busy as she was finishing her weekly shop this summer Saturday. She was at a 'credit card only' checkout machine, the end one of ten. There was a queue of mothers with tired children and fathers who were in a hurry, waiting for a free machine. Out of the corner of her eye, Sophie noticed a smartly dressed woman next to her, mid-seventies perhaps, like herself. She was wearing a pretty blouse, an orange summer skirt and a coral necklace. She was struggling to align the barcodes with the barcode reader.

People in the queue were sighing and one man said quite audibly, "Oh, *do* get on with it."

Sophie leant across and said to the struggling shopper, "Can I help?"

The coral necklace lady peered through thick-lensed glasses, with relief written all over her face, and said, "How very kind. I used to be able to checkout quite easily..." She stepped back a pace and allowed Sophie to complete the job for her. "Thank you so much. I feel embarrassed. Thank you again."

At the pedestrian crossing fifty yards from the shop, Sophie witnessed a near accident. An almost-silent electric bike, going much too fast, just missed a lady with an orange skirt. When Sophie saw who it was, she ran with her own trolley to accompany her from the traffic island to the pavement on the other side. The woman was trembling and shocked.

"Can I help you home?" Sophie asked.

"Well, that would be kind. But I don't want to take you out of your way. I should introduce myself," the woman said. "Mary Forbes-Robertson. Yes, I'm not far away at all."

As they pulled their shopping trolleys, they talked non-stop as is the way with people living on their own. They had both lost their husbands five or so years ago. Both were thrilled to discover they were painters in oils and were surprised that they hadn't met before. They bonded instantly.

Mary's house was the other side of the church from the town centre, down a short road and surrounded by well-tended, high hedges. It was a late-Victorian seaside villa. *Juniper House* was the name on the white-painted, wooden front gate from which a flagstone path lined with lupins and foxgloves led to a wisteria-covered porch and an oak front door.

Mary fumbled a bit with her key and Sophie hesitated to go any further, but Mary insisted that she should come in and have a cup of tea. The sitting room was exquisitely furnished. What immediately took Sophie's eye were the pictures – a dozen, at least – adorning the walls. Most were portraits in oil or of figures in movement and most were by Mary. To say she was accomplished would be an understatement. They were superb.

They chatted about Shoreham, about exhibitions (including their own) and about how awful Brighton had become. They showed each other recent completed pictures on their phones. Sophie had been specialising in flowers for years. But Sophie could tell there was something else, much more important, bothering Mary. She had been fiddling with a large magnifying glass for several minutes.

As Sophie got up to leave, Mary took her arm and said, almost pleading, "Don't go yet. I want to show you my studio."

The studio was a converted barn, a short walk down another flower-lined path – roses, dahlias and lilies – at the back of the house. It was unlocked. Canvasses of various sizes stood against three white walls. The fourth wall was a sliding glass door, through which Sophie could see another lawn with some gnarled trees, bent by the wind from the sea beyond them. There was the unmistakeable heady smell of turpentine, oil paint and varnish. There were several easels. A large one facing the glass door was surrounded by three tables with the usual artist's tools – brushes, a palette, tubes of paint and so on. It was completely covered by a dust cloth.

"I'm intrigued. What are you working on now?"

"It's a big commission. From a lady. I'm meant to be sworn to secrecy. I've told no one. But everything's changing now…"

She motioned Sophie to sit down in an old armchair and pulled up a stool beside her. She looked at the easel for several seconds. Neither of them talked.

"I'm sure I can trust you, Sophie. I'm a very old friend of hers. We go right back. She's a good correspondent and we've always kept in touch. A year ago, she asked me to do a picture based on this photo of them in their garden. It was to be for his birthday, a very personal present. Of course I accepted."

Mary carefully removed the dust sheet. Sophie gasped. The portraits were stunning and finished. But not the flowers. The couple were sitting in late afternoon light on a stone bench and the photo showed they were beside a large terracotta pot overflowing with snapdragons, pansies and nasturtiums.

"The problem is, Sophie, that I can't finish that side of the picture with that impressive Tuscan flowerpot and flowers. Apparently, he's very attached to that pot."

Sophie could see that Mary was struggling to hold back tears. She controlled herself and said, "Very suddenly, last week, my eyesight worsened; everything was distorted.

The eye hospital said it was something called wet macular degeneration; there was little they could do and that I could lose my sight in a matter of days…"

Without hesitation, Sophie said, "I'd be only too happy to do the flowers. They're my speciality. I could start tomorrow. After all, it's the way the Renaissance artists worked, isn't it? They often had others to finish their paintings."

The picture was completed by Sophie a fortnight later. It was beautifully framed in record time and just days before the birthday.

When the handwritten thank-you letter arrived addressed to Mary, she was completely blind. By chance, Sophie was visiting and she was able to read it to her. The sentence that gave them both special pleasure was: '*I particularly admired the way you captured the flowers, Mary. I can almost smell them. There's a nice story, too, about how I acquired the pots in Tuscany. Remind me to tell you when we next meet.*'

The embossed address at the top of the notepaper was simply 'Buckingham Palace' and the letter was signed 'Charles'.

A BIT FORGETFUL

For the month of August, I thought I would buy at least two books. I wanted to read books by authors that I had enjoyed in the past and would enjoy reading again. I've got rid of masses of books in London in a bid to declutter the house. I knew I would regret it. And I do.

Books have been part of my life. I'm glad to say printed books have seen something of a renaissance. Yet I'm amazed as I walk down the street at teatime in winter, before neighbours have closed their curtains, to see that many young people these days, in expensive houses, don't have any books – at least not on show. Perhaps they keep them upstairs.

I'm in pretty good health for eighty-three but my memory sometimes lets me down. It's not as good as it was. I don't think I've got full-blown Alzheimer's. I'm just a bit forgetful. The doctor keeps suggesting I take a test and I keep putting it off. I mean, I always know why I've gone shopping and I always remember whether I've locked the front door. Or almost always.

I'm keen to support independent bookshops. They've struggled against unfair competition on the internet. 'No names, no pack drill', as my father used to say. About ten years ago, a group of us got together to set up a bookshop to replace one that had sadly just closed. We had everyone's agreement to locate it – with the obligatory coffee shop – on the premises of our local library. But we hadn't foreseen that the borough council would knock the building down to build flats there. A new state-of-the-art library was built opposite. *Adieu* our lovely bookshop project, *adieu* our coffee shop with muffins and home-made chocolate cake and *adieu* our little limited company.

I reminisce. Now that I'm alone, I reminisce frequently. When I've spent a couple of days talking to myself, as well as shouting, "Nonsense!" or "Speak clearly, please!" at the newsreader on TV, I know it's time to get out more. My nearest bookshop is halfway between the house and the supermarket. They know me there and I can always have an intelligent conversation. Except I sometimes have difficulty keeping up. I do, at least, remember my name – William, or Billy as everyone calls me. And I remember the bookshop owner's name – Howard, or is it Henry? No, it's Howard, I'm sure.

"Morning, Billy," Howard said, as I pushed open the glass door.

"Morning, Henry," I said.

There were two other clients in the shop already: a blonde lady with a lovely smile, dressed in red from top to toe. And an older man with a fashionable beard, check shirt, smart trousers and suede shoes.

My eyes were drawn, as always, to the table in the middle

of the shop where Howard puts his selections of the week. I suppose he's obliged to have a few best sellers – pop stars' biographies, thrillers, spy dramas and science fiction. But Howard's heart is in the sort of niche books I like. This week there were half a dozen copies of *"Wet-on-wet; tips for watercolour artists."* A pile of *"Metal detecting for the professional"* with a cover photo of the actor whose tv series sent sales of metal detectors through the roof. And *"Unpublished short stories of Virginia Woolf"* which had a dreamy photo of the author taken when she was twenty-years-old. Howard had written little cards with his own frank appreciation of each book. *"Virginia Woolf was a great writer – but I can see why these short stories were unpublished. Too erotic for the 1920's".* A clever sales pitch.

After handling each of these books in turn – for a book must be handled, sampled, even smelt – I turned to Howard, who was opening parcels.

"I've reached a stage, Henry, I mean Howard, when I want to re-read the novels which have given me the most pleasure over the past, d'you know what I mean?"

"Of course I do, Billy. Classics are classics for a good reason. Though tastes change, don't they."

" Yes, they do. When I was in my late teens everybody was reading *"The Dam Busters"* or *"The Cruel Sea"* or *"The Wooden Horse"* – about war heroes. Odd really, because the one thing my parents wanted to do was to forget the war."

Thoughtfully, Howard had a stool for clients like me who were a bit wobbly on their pins and I sat on it. I noticed that the lady in red had picked up the Virginia Woolf book and was now searching the history shelf.

"There was a wonderful book about a man's dream of catching a big fish," I said.

"Moby Dick?" said the man with the beard who also had a copy of the Virginia Woolf under his arm.

"No. It was by another American, who was always boasting about how much he could drink."

"Hemingway," said Howard and the two clients in unison.

"'*The Old Man and the Sea*'" said Howard triumphantly.

"On the other hand, I'd prefer someone purely British," I whispered.

"My memory isn't much good these days, but I do remember Humbert Humbert."

"'*Lolita*'" said the man in suede shoes. This was becoming like a tv quiz show.

"But the author of that one was Vladimir Nabokov, American-Russian," said Howard.

"What about that wonderful writer with a famous brother – Lawrence Durrell, that's it, Lawrence Durell. *"The Alexandria Quartet."* Surely, he was English."

"Just," said Howard. "Born in India."

"Lived in France," said the woman in red.

"Four wives," said the man in suede shoes. As if that had anything to do with it.

I took a moment to reflect. I knew before I opened my mouth, that I was on the wrong track again when I said "'*Midnight's Children.'* Amazing manipulation of the English language, such a rich vocabulary."

"Salman Rushdie. Indian born. Half American," said the lady in red.

"Five wives," said the man in suede shoes disapprovingly.

I was now becoming desperate. Who was the most English of English? "Edward Fox," I blurted out.

"He's an actor," Howard said.

"Oh," I said. *"Day of the Jackal'* " by Frederick Forsyth, that's what I want."

Howard tapped on his computer again. "Re-printing. Won't be available until September."

The three others in the shop shook their heads. The man in suede shoes said, rather snootily I thought,

"Bad luck old man."

"Try Virginia Woolf," said Howard. "Short stories by great writers rarely disappoint."

THE CONVENIENCE STORE

J ames was funny, bright and kind, even as a child. To signal that he was toilet-trained, he put a potty on his head and marched around the house, banging on it with a wooden spoon. He blew into drinking straws instead of sucking and collapsed with laughter at the commotion it caused. When he was seven, he built a robot at school with a starter kit for ten-year-olds. The class bully smashed it up, hoping to reduce James to tears. James told him, "One day, you'll learn to be nice." The bully was expelled. James rebuilt the robot from scratch.

James' parents were loving but a bit too absorbed by their careers and hopeless with money. The mother was a special effects engineer at Pinewood Studios. Her income was erratic and she invested her savings badly. The father was an architect. His style was uncompromisingly modernist, minimalist and linear. His commissions were not as frequent as they could have been. The rented family home in Clapham was futuristic and clutter-free. All the family savings were spent on nursing home fees for their elderly parents.

When James was seventeen, both his parents tragically died, his mother of covid; his father, six months later, of a heart attack. James was adopted, as it were, by Mr and Mrs Rogan and their daughter, Lynne, who lived next door.

From that dreadful year onwards, James was determined to live positively. He inherited very little and abandoned his dream of university. His extravagance was to keep renting the house and, for this, had precious help from the Rogans. He took the first job he could find that didn't involve commuting. It was at the convenience store round the corner. Restocking the shelves, re-ordering and cleaning the shop were way below his intellectual capacity. At first occasionally, then more frequently, he was allowed to serve customers. His good looks, humour, kindness and intelligence proved to be a winning combination. He quite liked his nickname of 'Gentleman Jim'. The proprietor saw that he had found someone special. Footfall at the store doubled; sales, too.

There was a downside. Shoplifting became easier with more people milling around in the store, especially at lunchtimes and when the school day finished. It was mostly small packs of food and tins of alcoholic drinks that were stolen. When James saw that above a hundred pounds a day was being lost this way, he devised a super-rapid automatic door-closing system to trap offenders in the shop until the police arrived. Barcodes on goods that had not been paid for triggered the fast closure of the glass shop doors. Word soon spread that this was not a shop to be targeted; the problem subsided and, above all, James had an invention on his hands from which he could make serious money.

The Rogan family were greatly impressed by James'

invention. As it happened, Harry Rogan was an electrical engineer with a good knowledge of IT systems and his wife, Barbara, was an inventive kitchen designer. Within six months, James, Harry and Barbara had made a prototype, tested it, formed a partnership and applied for a worldwide patent. Lynne Rogan, just turned nineteen, found herself attracted to James almost without realising it. When drawings were spread out over the Rogan's dining table, Lynne's eyes were not on the paperwork. The attraction was mutual.

Lynne was as pretty as James was handsome. She was popular and James was flattered that she chose to date him. She was slightly shorter than James, had a glorious smile and an ever-so-slightly upturned nose. On summer evenings, they would play tennis on the courts on the Common. Lynne played well, hitting the ball almost as hard as James. When she served, her ponytail flicked up and James' heart missed a beat. After one year of her business and management course at Royal Holloway College, they married in the beautiful gilded chapel there – a song-filled ceremony accompanied by the college choir.

When the post office manager's job at the back of the store fell vacant, James applied for it and was chosen. The job gave him the security he needed. There was no commuting. All his spare time was spent on the glass-door project. Lynne was a valuable addition to the team. All that was needed now was a company to pick up James' idea, test it further and then manufacture it at scale. They pitched their project to companies and investors in the security, IT, shop-fitting and construction worlds. Eventually, they struck lucky with a security locks company in Sheffield – the largest in its sector. But the big company was nervous about the risk of installing a new production line; outsourcing the barcode recognition work; recruiting a new project manager. It wanted James to share the risk. It drew up a thirty-page draft agreement, which James and his partners found one-sided. So did their solicitor. It was a David and Goliath situation. After much negotiation, James agreed a deal under which he sold the licence to the Sheffield company, who would only pay once further prototypes had been tested and no earlier than in one year's time.

Meanwhile, James had incurred considerable costs. They included his solicitor, fees for an IT consultant, for industrial drawings, for the patent office, travelling expenses. Understandably, Harry and Barbara Rogan gave priority to Lynne's university fees and expenses. All this just as Lynne was desperate to make changes to the Clapham house, although she was not yet earning a penny. James secured two loans, one from a building society and one from his bank. Before long, he found himself in debt to the tune of £50,000. He knew he had over-extended himself and it gave him sleepless nights. But he never showed it at work. He went the extra mile with one client after another. He'd read that a Finnish philosopher, Frank Martela from Aalto University, had said that acts of kindness made for happiness. It acted as a universal language in a polarised world.

Disaster struck unexpectedly at the store's busiest time on a Friday at school closing time. From behind his post office counter screen, James saw a boy in a baseball cap calmly taking a half bottle of whisky, a six-pack of beer and a bottle of wine, and putting them in his backpack. As the thief ran towards the door, he tripped over a three-year old asking his mother for an ice cream. The toddler was sent flying, the mother screamed and James pressed the button for the police. The glass door slammed shut a second after being triggered by the barcodes, trapping the thief and his backpack in its grip. The doors had crushed his ribcage and punctured a lung. He was coughing blood when James released the doors while four male customers lay him on the floor, making sure he didn't try to escape.

The police came at the same time as the ambulance, but it was only in the hospital that they found he had a six-inch kitchen knife in his belt. The story, with video clip, was on that night's TV news and all over the social media. The Sheffield lock company took fright, suspended all work on the project and James' bank called in its loan.

Lynne was wonderful. She had heard nothing but praise for James' action from the local community. The police praised him, too, when announcing that a sixteen-year-old youth, arrested for shoplifting and carrying an offensive weapon in a public place illegally, would be appearing in court.

Lynne started a crowdfunding operation on the local WhatsApp platform and then on Facebook to pay off James' debts. She was overwhelmed with contributions and called a halt when the target was reached. Shoplifting was all over the news, people were generous and James had been lucky again.

As the Finnish philosopher also said: kindness is contagious.

SKETCHING
SUNSETS

The kitchen was in a mess when the two parents came downstairs. Dirty mugs, a slice of half-eaten veal and ham pie and an empty wine bottle had to be cleared away before Louise could make the coffee. Their son, Timothy, was already sitting at the kitchen counter with a glass of juice. He was red-eyed and looked older than his eighteen years. He had a sketchbook in front of him. James, the father, was in the same rumpled weekend clothes as yesterday. He was already answering an email on his smartphone but was able to mumble, "What a dreadful night." Louise brought three coffees to the counter. They all sat there for a moment in silence. Outside, it was going to be another hot day. The apples were fast ripening in the orchard.

Louise put her hand on her son's arm on the counter and held it tight. "Tell us again," she said in her soft voice.

"Grandpa and I," Timothy said, "had already sketched together twice this summer. He'd often said that the evening was the best time because of the skies and the fading sunlight through the trees. He said he'd always had his eye on the spot looking up to the ruined barn on Long Barrow Hill. We used to pick blackberries there years ago. Remember?

"After his siesta, Grandpa said he really needed some fresh air to clear his head. I suggested a bit of sketching together and he said that was a good idea. But could we wait until it was a bit cooler, so we fixed on popping out after an early supper, as you know. I suggested we take the car, but, of course, he insisted we walk. He stopped a couple of times, to listen to the woodpecker drumming on the hollow trunk of an oak.

"He's right about it being a good spot for painting. This side of the five-barred gate, with the lane at our backs, looking up the field, the old barn is silhouetted against the sky. There's the dark wood beyond and the hedges on either side provide a natural framing for a picture.

"We set the sketching stools side by side with our back to the lane. I could hear someone's tractor still at work in the distance. Grandpa has a routine. He unrolls the old piece of towelling that holds all his brushes and he lays all the brushes out neatly in descending size. On the other side of his stool, he puts his paintbox and water. Then, he looks for quite a while at the perspectives, where the horizon will be, the framing trees and the vanishing point. Then, he draws faintly but fast – never using a ruler, of course. He'd finished his drawing before I'd really started.

"'Come on, slow coach,' he said. 'This magical light won't last forever. Be quick with your pencil, lavish with your washes and bold with your colour.'

"We joked about the difficulty of drawing cows. He said he'd finish them at home later. The important thing was to capture the sunset. The clouds were amazing – ochre, orange, grey, pink and red. Grandpa said it made nature glow. He said many artists had tried to capture it but, in his view, only a few succeeded – Monet, Turner and some Americans. I can't remember their names now."

Timothy rubbed his eyes with his forefinger, swallowed his coffee and moved to the kitchen window. The lawn needed mowing. The cat needed feeding. And Timothy needed to talk.

"Grandpa saw I was struggling with the sky. I was trying to do a cerulean blue wash, but he said I had the wrong brush. Using his own flat brush and, with just a few strokes, he'd produced this effect." Timothy opened Grandpa's big sketchpad and touched the sky with the tips of his fingers. His father said it was wonderful. His mother said it was sublime.

"I was surprised that Grandpa didn't immediately go back to his stool. Instead, standing behind me, he squeezed my shoulders and stayed doing that for several seconds. The setting sun was just touching the line of trees at the end of the field. The faintest of breezes was warm and scented. The field in front of us was glowing and glistening with gorgeous greens. There was no more noise. It was as if nature was holding its breath. I suppose we were bonding with nature and with each other. It was special.

"He saw it first because, without saying a word, he pointed to the edge of the field where a majestic hare was sitting, then listening, then nibbling, moving closer and closer to where we were. It must have seen us but it wasn't frightened. It seemed to be enjoying the last moments of a hot day, probably too hot for hares, and was in a playful mood. It hopped, skipped and jumped, but kept its distance from the cows. Neither Grandpa nor I moved a muscle for fear of scaring the hare away. We must have remained like that for five minutes. It was as if this gorgeous animal had hypnotised us.

"Grandpa moved back to his stool. He had picked up his sketchpad and a brush, and I thought he was busy with his sky. I was desperately trying to merge my orange and pink clouds but my paper had dried already. The next thing I knew was that Grandpa was on his side, on the ground. His paintbrush was still in his hand.

"I turned him onto his back, shouted, 'Grandpa! Grandpa!' and slapped the sides of his cheeks. Then I saw his eyes. There was no life there. Still, I thought maybe if I gave him artificial respiration, or whatever it's called – you know, pressing with both hands on his heart. So, I tried that for about a minute, but it was hopeless.

"My own heart was racing by this time. Thank God I had my mobile phone with me and thank God there was a signal. I phoned 999 and told the operator that it was my granddad, that he was lifeless. I told them where we were, on the lane to Willow Farm. She told me to stay where I was – an ambulance was on its way. Finally, she asked how old Grandpa was and I couldn't quite remember. She said it didn't matter anyway and was I alright? I said I thought so. Then I rang you and you didn't reply because you were both at the bottom of the garden watching the sunset and didn't have your phones.

"I sat next to Grandpa on the grass verge and – it seems silly, I know – but I held his hand and talked to him. I said the clouds were entirely red now and the wood on the

99

horizon was black. I said the cows had come together a bit, had closed up, the herd instinct, which is what they do as night approaches. I said I would finish his picture for him and I would put his initials at the bottom of it.

"As I sat there and as it began to get dark, I looked up the hill towards the barn. I thought that this was the most perfect way for Grandpa to die. In the countryside he loved, painting a sunset. I should have realised that he wasn't feeling well when he stopped twice to listen to the woodpecker and then again when he was squeezing my shoulders. I couldn't see his face. Perhaps he was in pain then.

"And I thought how lucky, how privileged I was to be with him. I had a particular understanding with him. More than just friendship. Love, really.

"Then that hare popped up out of nowhere and came in a sort of zigzag almost within touching distance. It sat on its haunches, staring at us, with its big ears turning this way and that and its long whiskers. If hares could talk, it would have been saying, 'So sorry. Goodbye.'

"Then, the ambulance came."